WOLF'S SOUL
Guardians of the Fae Realms: Book 2
JL Madore

Wolf's Soul: Guardians of the Fae Realms

JL Madore -- 1st ed.

ISBN: 978-1-998372-59-1

CHAPTER ONE

Calli

$\mathcal{H}$e is our calming essence, our foundation, our spirit. To the four of us sharing the phoenix mating bond with him, he's Kotah, buddy, or Wolf. To the rest of the fae world, he's His Royal Highness, Prince Nakotah Northwood, heir to the Fae Prime, or, more recently, Fae Prime in Waiting.

Life sucks when you lose the right to choose.

In the week since I woke up the resurrected savior of the fae world on Earth, I would've been lost without my wolf. The youngest of the five of us, Kotah is the one with the old soul and most contemplative spirit. He's brilliant—fact, not hyperbole—and he's not even old enough to drink in a bar.

He's also an omega. From what I know, that's rare... like really rare. Not as rare as my human combustion on the side of a Texas backroad and rising from the ashes as a phoenix, but still rare.

"Hey, sweetie." I unbuckle my seatbelt and shift across the

middle bench of the SUV to get closer. Kotah is a stunning wolf wildling with Native American heritage. He's leanly muscled, with chestnut hair down to his very fine ass, and the sweetest, melt-you smile *evah*. And he's hurting—which hurts all of us. "Whatever happens, you're not alone. We've got you."

"Hells to the yeah," Jaxx says from behind us. The jaguar squeezes Kotah's shoulder from over the backrest of our seat. "We're a lock."

"Damn skippy," Brant, my grizzly says, turning in the shotgun seat to offer a wink. "There's no splitting up this band. We'll figure it out."

Even Hawk jumps on the reassurance bandwagon, offering a confident smile in the rear-view mirror. "No mate left behind, kid. Calli's right."

Kotah dips his chin and exhales. "It's the only thing making this bearable."

I snuggle against his side and lay my head against his chest. His heart races beneath my ear and for once, it has nothing to do with the crazy mating heat that has us all sexually keyed up and randy most of the time.

A wild growl rumbles from the front seat but it doesn't raise anyone's alarm like the guttural musings that Brant's bear usually does. That is his stomach.

"Hey." I point toward the front window of the truck at the roadside saloon coming up. Judging by the cars in the parking lot, it seems popular. "Any chance we can stop in for a burger and beer?"

"I could stretch," Brant says, straightening in his seat. "I'm in for a few brews."

"You're talkin' my language," Jaxx says behind me.

Hawk frowns. "We're twenty minutes from the Palace—"

"I'm in no rush," Kotah says, grabbing onto the lifeline. "I'd love a burger."

Hawk, our autocratic corporate raider, is cunningly efficient in all tasks. It may not have occurred to him beelining it straight at Kotah's worst fear isn't a good thing.

Trivial details like emotion and internal struggle don't naturally pop up on his radar.

"Kotah's the man of the hour," I say, pulling out my phone to call up my contacts. Since this is a brand-new phone given to me by Hawk it only has five numbers in it. My four guardian mates and Hawk's bodyguard and driver. "I'm texting Lukas to pull over."

Hawk pegs me with a look in the rear-view. He's got the whole intimidation thing down to a science, but this particular glance holds no heat. "Lukas works for me. Spitfire."

I shrug. "Done deal. He says, no problem. See, he's already hitting his indicator."

As our three-vehicle convoy sandwich pulls to the shoulder, the tires crunch over the loose-gravel lot. Lukas and Doc are in the lead truck with two FCO enforcers and they park away from the bulk of the other vehicles.

Hawk follows and pulls in beside them.

I lean back to fasten the top button of my jeans and then pull my shoes back on. "What time is it, anyway?"

Brant checks his utility watch. Hawk has one too. They are FCO-tech that do a heck of a lot more than tell time. They detect species of monsters, magical weapons, and other James Bond type things. "Almost four."

"Wow, it feels later than that."

Brant nods. "It's been a day, hasn't it?"

It has. After I shot a rogue drow murderer in the head at dawn, we flew to SoCal to clean out the apartment that, up until a couple of weeks ago, I shared with my best friend, Riley.

I didn't have it in me to pack up Riley's things. Her presence is still too strong around me to give her up for dead and move on. She's dead—I'm not in denial about that or anything—it's the moving on part I'm not ready for.

Thankfully, the guys saw that, and we changed gears. We gathered what I wanted, Hawk paid my landlord for the next two months, and we flew back to the Bastion.

Located two miles northwest of Lebanon, Kansas, the center of all fae law and administration is only one of the two most important centers found at the geographical heart of the continental United States. The other is the Prime Palace.

That's where we're headed now. Minus the pitstop at the burger joint saloon.

When the ride comes to a complete stop, Brant is quick to exit the vehicle and open my door.

"Thank you, Bear." I stretch as I drop to my feet outside, my muscles tight and stiff from lack of use.

Jaxx follows me out and does the same thing. "Damn, jaguars aren't meant to be crunched up in small spaces."

Brant snorts. "And grizzly bears are?"

He chuckles. "At least you got the front seat."

"Because I can't physically fit in the back."

"Semantics."

I smile inwardly. In such a short time, it's nice to see my guys starting to build genuine friendships. If we're meant to be a legendary quint of warrior lovers, we need a strong foundation. Mutual respect and friendship is a strong starting point.

I leave Brant and Jaxx to their banter and join Kotah and Hawk at the front hood. "Are we ready to head in?"

"Almost," Hawk says. "Lukas is doing a perimeter check while his team does a security sweep inside. Give them two minutes."

I roll my eyes but let Hawk play this out his way. He was cautious in the first few days worrying about me. Now that he knows Kotah's full identity as the blooded prince to the entire fae world, he's having a logistical meltdown.

I reach up onto my tiptoes and kiss his cheek.

He stiffens. I know he hates the contact, but that's half the fun. "Thanks for worrying about all the things so we don't have to. I appreciate it."

~

Hawk

The Rusty Spur is a county line watering hole fashioned after an old-west saloon. A long, wooden bar stretches the length of the left wall, there's seating near the front, an open dance floor further inside, and an upright piano sitting against the staircase. Those wide, wooden steps lead up to the second-floor mezzanine and the rooms upstairs. Saloon girls half-dressed in red silk skirts and black, thigh-high stockings lean over the railing from above and act as servers on the floor.

"Holy-schmoly, I love this place." Calli smiles as she makes short work of her bacon cheeseburger. "And the food is incredible. Here, try my rings."

Someone save me.

Of course, the Texan jaguar bumpkin and the farmer bear are in their glory. Calli seems to enjoy playing cowgirl, too. Unbidden, my mind shifts. Picturing her riding me cowgirl does nothing for my self-control. Fuck me. I scowl and adjust in my seat. "It's gauche and over the top."

Jaxx laughs and lifts the large, frosted mug to his lips. "You're the only one who thinks so, Hawk. Live a little."

I sigh and lift my fingers to count off my list of concerns. "The phoenix has risen. We were ambushed on the road because someone wants to do Calli harm. We're supposed to assemble an enchanted pendant but have no idea where the pieces are or how to find them. The kid is being recalled to take his place as Fae Prime. Until Calli's trained she's completely vulnerable—"

"Not completely vulnerable," Calli argues. "I took care of Plaid Nightmare and I held my own during the ambush."

Plaid Nightmare is her name for the human trucker who almost succeeded in raping her before a gang of drow took over and continued the sexual assault. I won't bring that up because even discussing it brings the four of us to violent rage.

The ambush, however, was a straight-on fight. "You were rocket launcher'd into a pond and almost drowned. But wait, there's more… I wasn't done with our outstanding issues."

I continue with the finger ticking. Since I'm finished my right hand, I flip to my left. "The Black Knight is moving behind the scenes amassing money for a purpose we haven't yet gleaned. My life and business are suffering every moment I'm not keeping my eye on the ball. And the entire fae realm is about to learn that their Prime is dying. Do you know how unstable that makes things?"

"Do you ever get a cramp in your tongue?" Brant asks, grabbing the handle of his beer stein and lifting the frosted mug to his lips. "My hope for all of us is that you someday find the end of your ramble of doom."

"Those are just the most pressing problems, Bear. Can you honestly look at me and say I need to live a little?" I toss back a dram of whiskey and repour with the bottle I bought for the table. "*Aaaand* ninety percent of the beer-guzzling nary locals set their sights on Calli as the exotic main attraction the moment she stepped through those tacky swinging doors."

"You can't blame them for that," Brant says, shifting his empty burger and fries platter under his newly arrived t-bone and baked potato platter. "Our girl's fucking hot."

"Aw, such a sweet-talking charmer," Calli says, before looking across the table at me and sobering. "You're right, Hawk. We need to nail down our daily training and our plan to find the gems. We need a lot of things, actually, and I'm sure more will pile up over the next few days. Just give us this moment to breathe and then we'll get back to it, I promise."

She offers me a sympathetic smile and tosses her napkin as the song changes. "Jaguar. I believe you asked for a dance last night that we never got a chance to take. Care to light the dance floor on fire?"

"Hells yeah," Jaxx says, taking another swig of his beer before rising to follow Calli onto the dance floor. Before he heads off, he chuckles and looks to us. "Seriously though, do we know where the fire extinguishers are? We don't want to light anything on fire and cause a scene."

As the two of them join the other three couples making spectacles of themselves on the worn hardwood, two-dozen gawking humans shift their gazes to follow our mate. I stretch my neck and fight the urge to kill them all.

Objectively, yes, I see why she draws attention.

Calliope Tannis is a full-figured blonde with gemstone green eyes and a kiss-my-ass attitude that's gotten her in and out of trouble her whole life. Squeezed into a pair of jeans with a plain white tank, she's about as down-home, pony-tail sexy as it gets.

And then there's her fire.

While mundane humans don't sense the magic of her phoenix or smell Jaxx's mating mark on her, their instincts pick up the dangerous lick of her fire. She possesses a raw power she doesn't understand or command yet.

It's alluring to both fae and humans alike.

She is the flame. They are the moths.

Except, I'm no one's moth.

I'm the fucking flame in my life.

Yes, her scent set up shop in my head. Yes, I've been hard and horny for days. But there's no fucking way I'm buying into this mating magic bullshit.

As Jaxx spins Calli on the dance floor, her laughter tightens the pain in my groin. I catch a gust of their mixed scents on the air and my hawk lets off a shrill scream.

The jaguar's mating mark on her flesh offends everything in me. Of the four of us, he's the one who's been inside her.

He's the one who she came apart for—

"Whoa, easy, Hoss." Brant's hand manacles my wrist and cuts off the circulation between my fingers and my Sig Sauer. "How 'bout you park your wagon and take a load off." He twists my gun out of my hand, his golden eyes glowing with the nearness of his bear. "This ain't the wild west and it's well past high noon."

What the fuck?

I stare at him, mouth agape as the world comes back into focus. Shit. I am getting dangerous. I wipe a rough hand over my mouth and meet Lukas's gaze at the next table. "I need some air. Walk me out."

∼

Kotah

With Hawk gone, Jaxx and Brant take turns dancing with Calli for the next hour while I watch. They wave me over to join them once in a while, but honkytonk new country isn't the kind of music the Prime Prince was taught to dance to. Not that it doesn't look fun—it does—but there's something more pressing occupying my mind.

When the rhythm slows down, I draw a deep breath and head out onto the hardwood. "Do you mind if I cut in?"

"Not a bit, buddy. Enjoy yourselves."

Brant steps away and Calli swings close and meets me chest to chest. A sexy sheen of sweat glistens on her forehead and her eyes glow bright like back-lit emeralds. I breathe her deep into my lungs, savoring her unique scent—it's feminine with the smoldering fire of her phoenix and the sweat of her exertions.

She feeds my soul. How is it, the universe thought I deserve such an incredible female?

"How are you doing?" she asks searching my expression as we sway close together. "I was hoping you'd change your mind and come dance your troubles away with me but if you want to leave, I'm sure Hawk can catch up."

Over the past few days, holding Calli has become my happy place. Her energy sings to my wolf, her scent fills my lungs, and her touch warms me to the marrow of my bones. If life could be this—the two of us holding each other close—I could live and die a content male.

Her breath washes the skin of my neck and raises the hair on my arms. The heat of her hand on my chest is the only thing keeping me from losing my nerve.

She eases back and my heart lurches. "Is everything okay? Your heart is racing."

"I'm panicked." My cheeks heat. "That has less to do with going home to my father and more to do with you."

"Anything in particular or me in general."

My body sways against hers, fear of rejection roaring in my ears. "Calli... I was thinking, hoping really... You see, I need... No, I suppose it's not a need. It's a want. It's definitely a want..."

She takes both my hands and clutches them between us. "Okay, stop with the warmup band and get straight to the main event. You think, hope, need, want what exactly?"

"You." My breath hitches and I swallow. "I want us to have sex. I want you to want me... to claim me before I go back there... to make it clear that I'm not the same boy who got shipped away because he'd never live up to expectations."

Calli stops dancing and her smile falls. "None of those are good reasons to give away your V-card, Kotah."

I close my eyes. "I shouldn't have asked. It's just... over the past week we've grown close. I adore you and I think the feeling is mutual. When I picture my future, it's you. And when we kiss, my whole world comes into focus. You're the one I want to be with. I know I'm young, but if I was ten years older or forty, it would still be you. My wolf may have been claimed by the mating magic, but you stole the heart of the male."

Her gaze softens as a smile spreads across her face. "Now, that is how you seduce your girl. Those are reasons I can get behind." She wraps her arms around my shoulders and brushes our lips together. "I'm not sure if you noticed, but there are a half-dozen rooms upstairs. And, if this place doesn't do it for you, Jaxx and Brant can drive us up the road to find a hotel. Whatever you want."

"Here's good," I say, glancing up at the wooden doors behind the upper railing. "Who do you think we talk to—"

"Hey, pretty lady." A man with a scruffy jaw and a black cowboy hat tugs Calli's shoulder. "How about you toss that minnow back into the pond and hook yourself a whopper? Never send a boy to do a man's job."

Calli

I twist out of the reach from handsy drunk number one and handsy drunk number two grinds up behind me. He's good enough looking that I'd bet he's used to his pretty face sealing the deal with women—not me, but other women. I smack his hand away from my ass and my phoenix rushes to the foreground. "Dude, unless you're my thong, you have no business crawling up my ass. Step off and mind your manners."

"You gave every other guy a chance to spin you around the dance floor. I'm just looking for equal time."

I take Kotah's hand and slide against his side. "Not interested. Buh-bye."

"You'd rather spend your night with a teenager? What I'm offering is all man."

I laugh. "And winning charm, right? Yeah, no. Sorry. I fail to see the appeal."

"Bitch."

"Says the drunken asshole."

He takes a swing and Kotah's hand flies up in a blur. My wolf catches drunk guy's fist and locks his hand mid-air. Kotah wolf growls long and low. Before the situation devolves, Brant, Jaxx, Lukas, and Doc form a wall at Kotah's side, cutting me off from the trouble.

Jaxx's turquoise eyes practically glow with the ascension of his jaguar. "Back it up boys. By the stench of alcohol seeping from your cells, you've had a busy day. You should leave now. You've officially overstayed your welcome."

The Clint Black wannabe pulls his arm free from Kotah's grip and flexes his fingers in and out. "We've overstayed *our* welcome? Listen blondie, we're regulars and you folks have never stepped foot in here before tonight. It's you who need to hit the road. Get out of our bar."

Brant chuckles, his broad shoulders blocking my view of everything happening on the other side of my protector wall. "Look, my man. Your cock got ahead of you and you overstepped. You propositioned our girl, she declined. End of. I'm ignoring the fact that you tried to hit her—mostly because it was so pathetic—but so far, no blood's been shed. Take the win and move on."

"Listen to him, Drake," a woman with a silver braid says from behind the bar. "Clear out for tonight. You haven't finished paying off the damages from the last fight you started."

"Don't worry, Clara. I got this."

"The only thing you've got is a choice to make, Drake," Jaxx says, tilting his head toward the bartender. "Option one, you listen to the lady in charge, apologize to Calli, and leave with your body parts and pride intact. Option two, you keep waving your big dick in the air and you wake up tomorrow morning with your nose broken wearing one of these silk corset and skirt ensembles, and your picture plastered all over the internet. You pick."

"Fuck you, pretty boy."

Kotah shifts me off the dance floor and over to the bar as the first punch flies. The scuffle is short-lived. Brant secures drunk one. Jaxx secures drunk two. And Doc, Lukas, and the five FCO security officers fan out quick enough, and look menacing enough, to discourage any other locals from joining in.

"Sorry about that," the bartender says. "Drake and his boys should've been cut off an hour ago. My new girl got suckered in by Paul's pretty face. Can I ask you to call off your boys and leave them in one piece? They're not bad guys, just bad drunks."

I shrug. "Don't kill them, guys."

Jaxx winks. "You got it, kitten."

I turn back to the bartender. "Okay, the drama is ending, everyone will remain in one piece, and your lovely establishment survived unscathed. Listen, as interesting as that wasn't, I'm wondering about your rooms. I'm feeling a little ill from the testosterone poisoning and want to call it a night."

The woman looks from me to Kotah and smiles. "I've got six rooms, all vacant at the moment. Each has a washroom shared with the room on the opposite side of it. The sheets are clean. The water's hot. The bar closes at one and will be noisy until then. Check out is eleven a.m."

I nod. "We'll take them all. I believe Mr. Barron gave you his credit card to keep the tab open?"

Clara nods. "An American Express Centurion. I never saw one before, but I checked and it's good."

"I have no doubt, it is. Look, these are good guys. We're not looking for any trouble, just a place to regroup for a few hours for a big day tomorrow."

Clara seems to consider that. "If you like, I'll have a couple of the girls come in at nine to fix up some breakfast. That'll be extra, but just to cover the groceries and their time."

"Perfect. Thank you." I pick up the six pistol keychains she offers and turn back toward the tables. "Just put everything on Mr. Barron's card."

CHAPTER TWO

Brant

"It's taking everything I have not to rip the cocks off these human asshats." I scowl at Jaxx as we do the drunk dick shuffle, my bear seriously offended. As a long-time player, I consider myself qualified in saying their man cards should be revoked. If there was a council or union of some kind for protecting the honor of dickdom, I'd be sending in my grievance.

"Strike one, assess the mindset of the female you're into, and only if she's open to what you offer do you proceed."

Nope. Fucked that up.

"Strike two, accept that rejection comes with the territory and if she's clear on her decision, bow out with grace."

Not even a little.

"Strike three, no matter how drunk you are or how badly you fuck up one and two, physical retaliation against the female is never—*ever*—an option. It's automatic disqualification not only to dating but to being considered men."

"No argument, Bear." Jaxx dumps flannel-guy onto the

asphalt and pulls a set of keys from his jean jacket pocket. He clicks the fob, scoops up his heap of unconscious asshole, and we head across the parking lot toward the corresponding *beep* and flashing lights.

Two loud *kerclunks* welcome these two bastards into the bed of the Dodge Ram. I check the saloon doors, happy to see Lukas and his guys have kept up their end and aren't letting the good ole boys inside join our party.

I hop into the driver's seat and start things up.

Jaxx points down the road the way we came earlier. "I saw a small church near the four corners of town. It had a lovely big bench out front. It'll be dark by the time we get there. I say, we flash off their clothes, flash on the saloon girl costumes, take a few pics, and get out of Dodge."

I hit the indicator and let the rumble of the engine lead the way. "I like the way you think, jaguar."

The tires eat up the distance as my mind drifts to the secret project I pulled Jaxx into. We don't get much time together away from the others, so I need to take advantage of the opportunity. "I made a call to a friend who oversees FCO expensing for the finance department. If Hawk's amassing a fae army of gifted super-soldiers, under the guise of being the Black Knight, I plan to follow the money to where he's hiding them."

Jaxx frowns. "Calli's going to be pissed if we go behind her back intending to trip up Hawk."

"This isn't about Calli. It's about Hawk and him using his position on high to destroy people's lives."

"And what if it's *not* him? What if he could help us figure out who is behind this? The faster we round up the Cavalry and circle the wagons, the better. I get that you don't like the guy—I'm not a fan either—but a powerful fae enchantment chose him to round out our quint. That means something."

"Was confiding in you a mistake, Jaxx? If you go to Calli,

she'll go to Hawk, and my investigation is stomped out before I figure out where those kids are."

Jaxx frowns. "I'm not goin' to anyone. I just want you to consider this from all angles."

"Tomorrow we'll be at the Prime Palace. The fae registry will provide answers. Let's keep things close to the vest for now and see what we find."

Jaxx rolls down the window and lets his hand ride the wave of the night air outside. "Fair enough. We'll hold off until we have more intel. I just don't believe a male who dedicates his entire life to the betterment of the fae can be the mastermind behind a Darkside plot. My gut says we're missin' the point."

Jaxx's phone beeps and he pulls it out to check the text.

"All good?"

He finishes reading and thumbs a response. "Yeah, the wolf wants to get laid before facin' his family."

"Smart kid. Not only the sex with Calli decision but moving up the status of his guardian position before his Prime calling becomes official."

"Yeah. Calli rented out the rooms above the bar for the night and is takin' care of business. We're invited to the afterparty. She left our key with Lukas. We're in The Stud room."

I snort. "Fuck yeah, we are. Was there any doubt?"

Calli

The Bronco, as our room is quaintly named, is simple, clean, and has a comfy bed. The shared bathroom is accessed through a little hallway that connects to The Stud, the adjoining room where I put Brant, Jaxx, and Hawk... assuming that when he comes back, he doesn't claim a room for himself. Which, who are we kidding, he will.

"There's a little porch out here," Kotah says, peering out the sliding-glass door. "The sun is almost completely set, but the sky is still lit up. Come see."

I join him, wrap my arm around his hips, and rest my cheek on his shoulder. The last of the sun's fire is glowing orange behind a mass of green treetops. It feels right to stand in his arms as we watch the light dim on a long day.

It already feels natural and it's only been a week.

What will life with these guys feel like in a year or over a lifetime? I catch myself and slow my mind down. Whenever I plan for a future, my world collapses, and the people I love are taken away. First, there were my parents, then my aunt, then Riley. Maybe I'm not meant to have a happily-ever-after. Maybe living in the moment is all I get.

I press a kiss to Kotah's jaw, and we watch as the sun sinks past the horizon. The sky swirls in pastel shades of pink, orange, and purple. It doesn't seem real. Too perfect.

Living in the moment is nice too. "It's pretty here... is it much like where you grew up at the palace?"

"I wasn't raised at the palace," he says. "My pack land in North Dakota is vast and densely forested with cave waterfalls and hot springs and wildlife in abundance. That is my home. I was brought to the palace to live with my parents after my sister and I were old enough to control our shifts and not embarrass them with our adolescence."

Embarrass them? My protective instincts kick in and I swear no one will ever make Kotah feel unworthy again. "Honestly, I'm sure you were happier there, living free to breathe in the fresh air. I can't imagine you stuck in a palace. I know how drawn you are to the wilds of nature's beauty."

"Speaking of nature's beauty," he says, turning, his gaze solidly toward me. "Thank you for this, Calli."

I tip my head back and brush my lips over his. "For getting naked with you? No sacrifice there."

His fingers sink deep into my hair. His raking touch sends sensation prickling over my scalp. "I meant for giving me the time to catch my breath before I face my father. But yes, for making a man of me before I do it, as well."

The most overpowering part of my new life isn't that four incredible males are mine for the taking. It isn't that I have a wild firebird burning inside me. It isn't even that a magical species believe I am their reborn savior.

No. The most overpowering part is the connection of skin-on-skin that zings through my cells whenever I touch one of them. It's breathing in the scent of sexual anticipation. It's knowing that if we get this right, this is forever, and none of us will ever be alone or wonder where we belong again.

I am determined to get it right.

"I love you, Calli," Kotah says, for once, not ducking his dark, brown gaze. We're almost the same height, so when he stares into my eyes, it feels like he sees behind all my barriers. "I know it's fast and you're dealing with too many new experiences to sort them all out, so I don't expect you to say anything back. I simply want to express what is in my soul. I love you."

Oh, my sweet prince.

I cup the smooth skin of his jaw and bring our mouths together. The sexual energy he emits as he meets my kiss is indescribable.

Unlike the heated frenzy of frantically fucking with Jaxx, Kotah moves slowly, savoring each touch, coaxing out the most succulent torture from me. His mouth. His tongue. His hands burrowing under my tank to splay against my heated skin. He makes my head spin.

Our mouths glide together in a mutual meeting of want, testing, and tasting. Heat and hunger stir and build in me, igniting a slow burn low in my belly.

My wolf is playful tonight.

His earthy scent fills my senses and the binding of our mating connection tightens. I feel the wounds scarring his soul. The rejection. The judgment. He needs so much more from me than a kiss.

"Kotah, do you trust me?"

"With everything I am," he breathes against my cheek.

Oh, my heart. I undo his jeans and push them down his powerful thighs. He steps out of them, yanking his shirt over his head and tossing it to the floor. My clothes don't last long either. In a tangle of groping hands and rucking garments, we stand together naked in seconds.

"I could kiss your lips forever," I whisper, hating to give up his mouth. I take his hand and guide him over to the bed, giving him a gentle push so he tips back and climbs onto the mattress. "But there are other parts of you needing attention."

I prowl up the bed on my hands and knees. Kotah's gaze locks on the sway of my breasts and a low growl rips from his throat. He catches me watching him and his gaze skitters away as his cheeks flush.

I straddle his hips and sit on his abdomen. Taking his hands, I bring them to cup the weight of my breasts. "Don't be embarrassed about liking the girls. They like you, too."

His thumb brushes over the peaked point of my nipple and I show him the pressure I like for a gentle pinch and twist. His touch sends a zing of pleasure straight to my core. "They're yours now, too. Don't be shy. Get to know them."

We spend a few more minutes with him teasing the tight buds and me arching into his touch before I open my eyes and check on him. "You doing okay?"

"You honor me, *Chigua*. I have been lavished with priceless gifts my entire life, but you are, by far, my most precious treasure."

I collapse forward to kiss him. "Okay, talk like that deserves a reward." Lifting my hips, I slide to the side and wriggle down his thigh. "One thing you should know about me, Kotah. I love sucking cock. I hope you're up for it."

A groan rasps from his throat when I drop my head and he tenses. "Calli... I don't know how much... I mean, I want to be good at this, I just don't..."

My lips part over Kotah's cock and I suck his shaft deep into my mouth.

"Oh, *sweet powers!*"

I chuckle. I made my prince utter an expletive. Well... it's an expletive for him. Well-mannered and trained in social expectation, it seems I jolted him out of his comfort zone. Good. That's what I was going for.

The taste of him, sweet and salty, laces my tongue. I suction around his shaft and start a slow bob from the rounded head down toward the base of his pelvis.

Kotah fists the covers and his abs start to clench. His skin is hot and smooth in my mouth, gliding over the solid shaft of his erection. I pause at the top of my stroke and swirl my tongue through the pearly cream weeping from his slit.

"Calli..." He flexes forward, gripping into the back of my hair, urging me away from where I want to be. "I'm sorry. I'm not going to last. You should—"

I refuse to lose out on sucking him off to release. I ignore his urging and double my efforts. When his breath hitches and his hips start convulsing, I devour him. Warm, salty cream hits my tongue and I groan as I swallow it down.

Maybe it's something to do with the mate marking or maybe it's a wildling thing, but I swear his cum feeds my phoenix. My power surges inside me, the fiery animal within reeling in the pleasure of my mate's pleasure. I suckle and swallow, licking every last drop Kotah gives me.

"You taste good, my prince."

Kotah groans. "That's not what I had in mind. I wanted to be inside you, Calli. I wanted—"

I laugh and crawl higher on the bed to lie with him. "You said you trust me, so have faith. All we did is take off the edge of adolescent anticipation. We have this room for the whole night. By dawn, you will be drained dry and so incredibly sexed the guys might have to carry you into your father's compound."

His growl vibrates through me and makes my clit throb. "Yes. I want that. I want there to be no doubt that I'm yours and that you claimed me as your guardian."

I run my hand between his thighs and palm his balls. His cock twitches on his abdomen and stirs back to life. "Your orgasm isn't an ending, Wolf, it's a beginning. When I'm finished with you, no one will question that you are mine or that I am yours. I promise."

∾

Kotah

Calli is a marvel. I thought her captivating and beautiful before but when she looks up at me with affection in her eyes and her skin glistening in a light sheen of sweat we made with the friction of skin-to-skin, I'm at a loss.

"I love you," I say, my voice deep with affection. I know I keep saying it, but I can't help myself. I press my hand over her stomach and caress a path up to meet the rising mounds of her breasts. She teased me earlier, but there's no denying how much I covet her breasts.

I cup them, kiss them, pay homage to the tight buds of her nipples with my mouth, my tongue. Her skin is soft and pliable beneath my cheeks and chin.

Shifting to wolf for night runs and swimming in the natural pools has given me ample opportunity to inventory the female physique. Calli is different from any female I've seen. The she-wolves of my pack have hard, ridged stomachs and the small breasts of slender, muscled females.

Calli is succulently soft, and full-bodied. Her breasts conform to my hold, her belly tender. I handle her breast the way she showed me and my wolf growls as her arousal blooms.

The way she responds to my touch is magical.

It's a gift.

I meet her gaze and the amusement dancing in her eyes makes my cheeks flush hot. "Apologies. My staring is making you uncomfortable, isn't it?"

"Not at all, sweet prince. This is your night. You get to ogle and touch and explore as much as you like. What's at the top of your wish list right now?"

To mount you and mate you. I blush. I can't say that.

She chuckles and brushes the heat of my cheek. "Whatever came to your mind, my answer is yes."

My erection pulses between us and I take the hint. As I roll over her, she opens her knees to make space for me in the cradle of her hips.

I meet her eyes. "Am I hurting you?"

"Just use your hands or elbows on the mattress to take some of your weight off me.

"Apologies." I shift my weight as quickly as I can and raise onto my elbows. "I want to be good at this. I want you to value me in your bed. I want—"

She presses her fingers over my lips and smiles. "Don't over-think it. Sex is largely about sensation. If you're all up in your head, you'll lose your drive. I promise I'll let you know if something isn't working. You can do the same. Now, didn't you say you want inside me?"

I swallow, less sure of myself than ever.

She undulates her hips and pulls me closer to claim my lips. The heat of her hands running the length of my spine brings me back to focus. She urges me higher and the heat of her entrance meets my swollen tip. Her moist folds are hot and wet against my flesh.

"Sweet powers, that feels good."

She bites my lip and my wolf prowls forward. I meld our mouths, taking possession, our lips moving as one, our tong—

Calli groans beneath me and I freeze.

I've pushed inside her. I break our kiss and my body shudders with bombarding sensations, the heat of her core, the grip of her inner muscles, the moist glide when I move even the slightest bit.

"Breathe, Wolf."

Breathe, right. I draw a deep breath and commit this moment to memory. Not that I think I'll ever forget it but—

Calli reclaims my mouth and her hips start to move.

"I think my heart might burst," I gasp, understanding that the motion of her hips is her body urging me to take the lead. I do. After a few strokes, I adjust to the sweet depths of her. After a few more, I increase the speed and strength of our joined in and out motion. The penetration, the stretch, and squeeze, the wet friction...

Magic igniting inside Calli triggers my empathic gift.

It courses between us, swirling from Calli into me and back again. It's our mating bond. It's tightening. The connection that links us is stronger. Where before it was rope, it's now a steel cable. The two of us bound in an unbreakable link.

Yes. Her phoenix calls to my wolf as fire licks over my skin. It's hot but doesn't burn. It's a sexy welcome from her wildling side, a forging of two mates.

My breath hitches and the pressure building in my sac burns hotter. I want to mark her but I don't want this to end. Not tonight. Not ever. At this moment I don't know how I'll ever survive if I'm not inside her.

"Oh, gawd," Calli gasps, writhing beneath me. "Harder. I need more of you, all of you."

A low growl vibrates from my wolf. It's a primal sound and I understand what she meant by sex being largely sensation. I allow my wolf to ascend more and his aggression and possession embolden me.

I thrust harder and faster, fully penetrating her. Where I worried about hurting her, giving hard thrusts brings both of us even more pleasure. Her knees come up and I hook them around my elbows, pinning her open. Holding power over her pleasure like this feeds the wildness in me. It's empowering to hold her so tightly, to have her trust me with her body.

I'm no longer making love to Calli, this is more—much more. And as crass as it sounds, hammering into her blows my expectations of sex with her to bits. We're dripping in sweat, our skin slicked together, our chests heaving for air.

Calli cries out and her release explodes across my empathic connection. Everything in her tightens and clenches, squeezing. It's total surrender. It's chaos. It shatters my mind and my understanding of everything I thought I knew.

Now it's me who's losing control. I throw my head back and shudder, coming inside her so violently, I wonder how mates survive this much pleasure.

CHAPTER THREE

Hawk

I read the text from Calli and curse. Join them for the sexual afterparty? No way. My hawk is so wild and out of control, I almost drew my gun and went after Jaxx in the middle of a human bar. Well... I *did* draw it, but for once, Brant proved himself useful and pushed into a situation when and where he was needed.

I hang my head and breathe in the pungent scent of fir needles. Spreading my wings for a few hours helped but sitting out here on this branch in the middle of nowhere isn't touching the pull on my soul to return to my female.

Every instinct I possess screams inside me. I need to be at Calli's side. I need to press inside her and accept my fate as her mate. There's no way I can hold back the deluge of mating magic if the other four are naked and sexed up.

I touch my lips and shudder. Despite Calli's kiss still singing on my lips from last night, there's no way I'm joining the mating frenzy.

I swallow and look down at the party in my pants. "Sorry, big guy. You're benched for the foreseeable future."

My phone rings in my hand and I check the ID. My heart lurches into my throat and chokes my breath. "Lukas? What's wrong? Is Calli all right?"

"She's fine. They all are." There's no waver in his tone. My hawk eases. "The young prince wasn't ready to face his future. She took him upstairs and retired for the night. I assume she texted you?"

"Did Jaxx and Brant join them?"

"No, they went to town on an errand."

My dander raises and my hawk ruffles its feathers. "They left her and the prince unprotected? What the fuck is wrong with them? What could be more important—"

"There was an altercation with two drunken humans."

"*What?* Why didn't you call me?"

"I just did."

I drop from the branch twenty feet off the forest floor. The impact with the forest floor jars my sore knee. "Don't get flippant. You know what I mean. What if she needed me?"

"I'm sure she does, Barron, just not to defend her from two intoxicated rednecks. She had three other guardians, the bear doctor, and the five of us. All is well."

I close my eyes and study the full, pearl moon through the web of branches above my head. I'm failing. In my duty as the head of FCO and, at the same time, in my role in the quint. Even if I refuse the mating, or cut the binding, I still want the four of them to be safe and strong and supported.

With that in mind, I see my next move. "Since you have things well in hand, I'm taking point. I'll head to the palace to prepare for your arrival in the morning. Text me when the others return and settle in for the night."

"You're not coming back?"

I ignore the censure in his tone. "Divide and conquer. Call me if anything untoward arises. Otherwise, check-in with me in the morning. And Lukas... take every precaution with them. Keep them safe."

"Of course, sir. Good night."

Kotah

It's close to ten o'clock when a knock sounds on the door to the adjoining hall. The bass thrumming through the walls from the bar almost drowns it out, but with heightened wilding hearing, neither of us miss it.

"Anyone up for some mate company?"

My heart leaps at the sound of Jaxx's voice. Am I ready? Will I ever be ready? Even if the males remain solely focused on Calli, am I ready for witnesses to my inadequacies?

Calli says I'm a natural, but I do not doubt that both Brant and Jaxx are exceptional lovers. Hawk, too. Oh, sweet mercy, is Hawk back? Will he be here too?

Calli lifts her head, her arm draped across my navel, her half-masted gaze one of sated bliss. I did that. I put that smile on her lips. "It's up to you, sweet prince."

"Yes." I draw a deep breath and pull the sheet across our lower halves to give Calli a bit of modesty. "Come join us."

Jaxx is bare-chested, barefooted, and wears only his ripped jeans. His golden skin shifts back and forth over coiled muscles with each step closer. "You good, buddy? This is your night. If you want to call dibs and hunker down for a quiet night, there's no fault no foul. Just say the word."

As tempting as that sounds, I shake off the impulse.

"Jaxx is right," Brant says, taking up the rear. He's wearing the sweatpants he puts on at night for Calli's benefit and a tight black t-shirt. "It's your call, Wolf."

A pang of need twists in my gut. It isn't sexual—it's more. It's something new to me. It's a need for a deeper connection with my mates. "As you said, Bear, with five of us, there are lots of possibilities for entertainment, right?"

"True story."

I agree. "I'm good with you guys sharing our bed. I'm just not giving up my spot. I recently suffered heart failure and haven't recovered enough to move yet."

The bass of Brant's laughter reverberates in my chest. "Well, then. It's good to know our girl christened your manhood with gusto."

Now it's my turn to laugh. *Gusto?* Sweet mercy.

My cheeks flush hot and I glance down at Calli. Her eyes are closed. I watch her lying there limp. Her breath saws in and out in soft gusts.

Jaxx follows my gaze and a loving smile washes over his face. He drops his jeans and slides into bed behind her. "She looks well and truly sated, pup. Well, done. Let's let her sleep. Early to bed it is."

Brant eyes the bed and shakes his head. "If sleep is the plan, I'll be next door in the Stud bed."

Jaxx spoons Calli and covers us with the blanket. "You were just dying to say that, weren't you?"

Brant laughs and waves over his shoulder. "Hells yeah. Wake me up if anything exciting happens."

Calli

A shift in the sheets stirs me from my warm cocoon of slumber. I stretch, arc my back, and assess all my fabulously tender girly parts. Being with my wolf last night was a gift. After my disturbing start with sex, I waited years before trusting someone enough to be intimate. I missed the nervous and awkward phase of learning what two inexperienced bodies could do together. I missed the innocent joy of simply marveling at the sensations.

Kotah gave that back to me.

The scent of him fills my mind and when I open my eyes, I find his wide, chocolate gaze glittering inches from mine. There's a look of raptured amazement on his face. It's simple and natural and I'm so thankful to have him in my life.

"Good morning," I say, closing the distance between our mouths. "How are you feeling? Any awkward 'morning after the night before' moments we should address?"

He shakes his head, his hair cascading around his bare shoulders, wild and long. "I'm blissfully content."

"Excellent. Me too."

Jaxx presses up behind me and kisses my shoulder. "Our boy wore you out last night. When the bear and I came to check-in, you were sawing logs like a buzzsaw."

I giggle and sink back down to the pillow. "Nice try, puss. I don't snore."

His million-dollar smile fills my heart. "We wouldn't care if you did. Waking up with you is worth any price we have to pay, isn't it, kid?"

Kotah's smile tightens. I sense the sting of something below the surface and it speaks to my new wilding instincts. "Hey," I say, running a hand down his smooth, bare chest. "What happened there? Are you okay?"

"Yes, of course. Aside from never wanting to leave this bed, what could be wrong?"

It's true, with his homecoming on the horizon he's bound to have a few things pressing on his chest, but the discomfort I feel is more immediate. "Okay, rule number one of our mating bed.

This is our safe place. We speak our hearts here. There's no wrong answer and I'll never question you or judge you on anything we share."

His shy grin tells me he remembers speaking those exact words to me two days ago when he began teaching me to connect with my phoenix.

I tease my fingers over his nipple. "Something hurt you just now, what is it? What do you need?"

He looks like he might balk and fake that he's good, but then his smile falters. "I'd like a lover's nickname that isn't kid or buddy or pup or anything to do with me being younger than all of you. I face my father in a few hours and want my community —and honestly the four of you—to see me as the male I see myself to be."

"Of course, baby—crap, sorry. I'll work on that."

"Shit, Kotah," Jaxx says, reaching over me to squeeze Kotah's arm. "I'm sorry, my man. Yeah. That's reasonable. I never meant—"

"No. I know you didn't," he says, sitting up. "I'd simply rather you four address me with an endearment that doesn't reflect me being too young to understand what the grown-ups are talking about. I fight that stigma every day and it's exhausting. With you I want to be me—one of the quint."

My heart aches for Kotah, and I pull him into a full-body hug. I kiss him and it's soft and sexy. "I'm glad you spoke up. And this quint is blessed to have you. Does it bother you that I call you my sweet prince? Do you want me to stop?"

He arches a brow and blushes. "No. I like the way you say that. And after last night, it'll remind me of some very fond private moments."

I bite my lip and just like that, my sex-drive revs and is ready to roll. "You deserve many more of those moments."

Jaxx nods. "And honestly, dude, when I look at you, I don't see a young boy or the Prime's heir. I see an off-the-charts smart guy, with a ripped and rockin' body, and a pure spirit that will surely point the moral compass of our quint for years to come."

Kotah's pupils widen as the two of them get lost in a stare. I glance from Jaxx to Kotah and back again. "Okay, did the sexual energy in this bed ratchet up ten notches, or am I imagining it?"

Jaxx slides a sly smile at me. "And what if it did, kitten? What do you think we should do about it?"

I bite my bottom lip and lean back with my arms behind my head. The position lifts my breasts and both guys get distracted admiring the girls. "Then I think Kotah could use a bit more quint love before he faces the harsh world of the Prime. I think my guys should kiss."

Jaxx's chest bounces as he pegs me with a playful look. "Are you turned on by male on male, kitten?"

"It's a very new interest. Let's try it out and see."

Kotah rises to his knees on one side of me and Jaxx mirrors the position on my other side. They're both gloriously naked and I don't know if it's morning wood or my request that has their cocks solid, but… it's *waaay* too sexy to care.

Jaxx is the alpha and takes control. His fingers slip into Kotah's chestnut hair, holding his head in place. Leaning forward, he fuses their mouths and they meet, chest-to-chest, right above me.

Hubba—wow.

My body falls under their seductive spell. My skin tingles, my nipples tighten, and my throat goes dry.

Kotah is omega but isn't submissive. He grips Jaxx's ribs, his fingers digging into the golden flesh of my jaguar. There's so much to take in, flexing abs, bumping cocks, morning-scruff mouths moving as they kiss the hell out of each other.

"So hot." A rush of heat hits my core. I reach between them with both hands and take possession of those erections. They kick and press into my hold. A wave of dizzy washes over me at the same time my arousal weeps between my legs. "Ohmygawd, *sooo* hot."

Jaxx's purr fills the room. The bastard. He knows what that does to me. An achy tension builds low in my belly. I watch the flex of muscles beneath their chins as their tongues battle for supremacy.

This may have started as a show for me, but it is morphing into full-on male passion. I squeeze my grip, stroking them off. "Gawd, I'm so turned on by you two right now. Don't stop. Please don't stop."

I breathe deep, my animal senses bombarded by the spicy mark of mating on my skin, the musk of Jaxx, the earthy scent of Kotah, and... my bear.

I swing my gaze toward the adjoining room.

Brant has turned the upholstered chair near the door to face the bed and is sitting, man-spread and naked. He's gripping a very impressive erection and stroking himself while taking in the show. His half-masted gaze is heated and possessive. He winks and a fresh wave of moisture dampens me.

Mine, he mouths.

His cock slides through his fist, glistening and proud. He's beautiful—and massive—the muscles of his arm, pecs, and abs rippling with power.

My breath stops. Need shoots from my mind, straight to my empty core. I need him inside me. I want—

Kotah growls and I remember to stroke the two of them.

The sight of the two of them making out is the sexiest thing I've ever seen. The groping hands. The desperate connection of chests and hips. Biceps bulging with their grip on one another. The growls and groans as their passions leak onto my hand.

I use their pre-cum to slick their cocks and jack them faster. My pussy tightens, my release aching at the edge of my control. "Come on me," I say, unsure from where the need stems. "Slick me. Mark me, boys."

Kotah throws his head back and his abs convulse. His hips thrust forward and the muscles in his neck strain so tight I'd swear they might snap. Creamy jets spurt free and fall to warm my breasts and belly.

It's exactly what I asked for and exactly what I need.

Pleasure shoots from my nipples straight to my core and I topple into an abyss. I release their cocks and arc off the mattress. Pleasure grips me and I'm lost in sensation as my world falls away.

"*Dayum.*" Jaxx's purr rips from his heaving chest. He grips Kotah's shoulder as our wolf takes over stroking him off. Our jaguar doesn't last. He throws back his head, his release splattering Kotah's thigh and adding to the mess pooling on my breasts.

I sweep my hands through the cream, loving the mix of scents. Everywhere their cum touches me, my flesh heats up, energy explodes off my body, and fire licks over my skin.

My body ignites in full glow.

I'm ramping up fast for another explosion. "Someone get inside me. Please, I need to be filled."

One beautiful thing I've learned about wildlings is their sexual refractory time is almost non-existent—the room spins as Jaxx takes control.

He flips me onto my knees and is on his back and between my thighs in a sixty-nine. "Kotah, take her from behind while I lap up her cream."

I cry out as Jaxx sucks my clit into his mouth and Kotah penetrates me from behind. "Yes! Oh, gawd, yes."

My legs quiver and I lose track of where I end, and they begin. Nothing in life prepared me for this. I don't know why the universe chose me but don't ever want to go back.

The wet slap of flesh on flesh with Kotah pumping inside me and the bruising force of Jaxx's fingers holding me steady while he tongues me... it's too much.

I shatter. My second orgasm takes me out of my body while everything I ever thought I knew about myself bursts apart. Skin alight and tingling... breath shallow and heaving... mind blown and spinning...

... and I plummet into a black abyss.

CHAPTER FOUR

Jaxx

*T*he world is a perfect frenzy of pleasure until Calli goes limp in my grip. Deadweight in my arms, she hits my chest and my heart stops. "Calli? Calli, what's wrong?" Kotah pulls back, panting as I shift out from under her and roll her to the mattress. "Kitten? Open your eyes. What happened? Where'd you go?"

Years of first responder training kick in and I shift modes to assess her. Pulse: rapid but steady. Pupils: responsive. Breathing: shallow but strong. Skin: sweaty but that means nothing...

"What happened?" Brant snaps, suddenly at the side of the bed. The bear is naked and by the scent of his skin was enjoying a sex party of his own making.

"She passed out," I say, praying I'm right. "Thirty seconds ago, she was buckin' like a bronco and lit like a torch aflame. Then another orgasm hit, and she crashed."

"Does that happen?"

"It can... though it's not common."

"She's waking up." Kotah clutches her hand and brings her

knuckles to his lips. Her hair is matted to the side of her face with sweat and he peels it back. "*Chigua*, are you well?"

She blinks a few times, her gaze roaming and unfocused.

"Calli, look at me," I say, holding my finger up in front of her face. "Focus, kitten. Do you know where you are?"

Her face scrunches when she frowns. "What happened?"

"You fainted," Kotah says. "Are you all right?"

Her frown smooths out and she brushes a gentle palm against his cheek. "More than all right, sugar. You guys blew my mind. I've never orgasm-fainted before. Is that a thing?"

I drop on the bed beside her and pound my chest. "Yeah, and it scared the shit out of me. So, that's what a heart attack feels like, eh?"

"Sorry. It's your fault too. You boys broke me."

I take a deep breath and try to let the panic go. "Kotah, how about you warm the shower and we'll get our mate clean. Brant, can you get dressed and see if Doc is up for a house call in ten?"

"Done deal," Brant says, joining Kotah on the way to the little hall joining the two rooms.

"Guys, I'm fine, I swear," Calli protests. "Come back to bed. Don't worry about me."

Too late for that.

When we're alone, I check her pulse again. "Seriously, Calli. Is there anythin' you didn't say because you're embarrassed or want it kept private? Health concerns from before your transition. Symptoms you might've been avoiding since you woke up reborn. Anythin' at all I should know about."

She sits up and presses a chaste kiss on my lips. "No, puss. The sex blew my mind and here we are. Gear down your panic train and park it in the station. Today is Kotah's day. Focus on him, 'kay? I'm all good."

∽

Hawk

I open the back door of the middle Suburban when the phoenix and her mates arrive mid-morning. There's little fanfare. Nakotah didn't want a formal reception upon his return to the Prime Palace, so I honored his wishes and made the arrangements discreetly through Raven, the head of house for the royal family. "Welcome home, kid."

The wolf gives me a tight-lipped nod and steps out of the truck. Calli scoots out behind him, accepts my hand, and hops down from the truck. I stare at our joined fingers, letting the power of that simple connection ease the raging storm waging war inside me.

It galls me that I hated being separated from them last night. I laid awake staring at the architectural molding along the ceiling line, counting the cut crystals in the chandelier, and focused on not needing a female to complete the male that I've become. It was futile bullshit.

"Hey, there." Calli tightens her fingers around mine and stretches up to kiss me.

I shift quickly enough that her lips settle on my cheek and step back. Her scent is altered again. She had sex with both Jaxx and Kotah now, and by the strength of their mating mark, very recently. I gird my fury and swallow my possessive instinct past the bile burning my throat.

"Lukas informs me that you had some trouble with the locals at the bar last night. Are you all right?"

"Fine." Her brow pinches. "You look tired, Barron."

I am. The past week has been a blur of sleepless nights and stressful days. When I stare into those expressive green eyes of hers, I want to give up the battle and admit defeat. I want to fall into whatever destiny has in store for us... but I won't. *I* choose my destiny. Only me.

"No rest for the wicked, I'm afraid."

Lukas finishes speaking with the security team and they drive off to park the vehicles. Jaxx gives Brant and Kotah a private glance and they join us with some unspoken purpose.

"If you don't mind," Kotah says, taking Calli's hand from mine, "I'd like to give Calli a tour of the palace and introduce her to a few people. Can we meet you back at our suite after that? I assume Raven set us up in one of the resident suites in the east wing."

I take the cue and nod. "We're in the Timber Trail suite. See you then."

The moment Kotah and Brant whisk her into the palace, I turn to Lukas, Jaxx, and Doc. "What happened? And why don't you want Calli to know you're talking to me about it?"

Lukas scowls. "I'm unaware of anything—"

Jaxx licks his lips. "No offense guys but could you give Hawk and I a bit of privacy?"

My heart rate ratchets up a million notches. Lukas looks alarmed. I raise my palm. "It's alright. Give us a moment."

When I'm left to speak privately with Jaxx, I lock down my tension and wait for him to fill me in. Lukas mentioned nothing, so I know the trouble likely doesn't involve Calli's safety but by the look on Jaxx's face, it's no less dire.

"There's no delicate way to put this, so I'm just getting' it out. This morning, Calli, Kotah, and I were havin' one hell of a threesome session. When our girl hit her last climax, she collapsed in a dead faint. I checked her vitals and she seemed fine but I don't like it."

I scrub a rough hand through my hair and realize why Brant's doctor friend is pacing around on our periphery. I wave him over. "The two of you have obviously spoken about what happened, so what do you think?"

Doc, the ursine black bear who, over the past four days, has become our unofficial guardian physician frowns. "It could be as simple as her swooning. Both Jaxx and I have examined her since, and she seems fine."

"But what are the causes of something like this if she's not fine?" I ask. "I've been with hundreds of women and not one of them has ever lost consciousness unintentionally."

Jaxx frowns. "How many of those were human?"

"None. I've never had a taste for the race."

Doc nods. "Being a military medic, I've treated patients from all races. And while human physiology isn't divergently different from some fae races, some of their frailties do warrant our concern."

Done deal. I'm *very* fucking concerned. So concerned, my hawk is about to burst out of my skin. "Do you think it was simply her fainting? And if not, what are you saying?"

Doc's expression tells me nothing. My fucking superpower is reading people and I've got nothing. "I think, for the moment, we need to ignore Calli's protests and look deeper. Yes, maybe she became so sexually aroused that her breath quickened too rapidly. That could disrupt her body's balance of carbon dioxide and oxygen and make her lightheaded."

"What else could it be?"

"Vasovagal syncope, for one," Doc says. "That's when the vagus nerve running from the brain to the chest and abdomen becomes overstimulated. It causes a drop in heart rate and blood pressure and can lead to brief unconsciousness. Or it could be postural orthostatic tachycardia syndrome."

Fuck, that sounds bad. "In layman's terms?"

"It's a big term that means she switched positions too quickly and the low blood volume making it back to her heart caused her to pass out."

Jaxx looks stricken. "I did flip her from her back onto her knees rather quickly."

Images of Jaxx handling Calli roughly fill my mind and the dagger-sharp tips of my talons pierce the nailbeds of my fingers.

I'm back to my hawk's instinct of last night when I wanted to slay Jaxx. Perfect.

I turn my attention to the bear. "What else?"

"The only other thing I can think of would be an abnormal heart rhythm."

I curse. "So, the strength and health of her heart are involved in any of the scenarios."

Doc's gaze is full of sympathy. "Calli could be right. She might've been overwhelmed and hyperventilated during her last orgasm."

Last orgasm. How many releases has she given the jaguar? And now the wolf?

"That's what she says happened," Jaxx says, "but I'm not willin' to dismiss it. Not when it could mean her life."

"Agreed." I rub a rough hand through my hair. "You have our next steps thought out, I presume. Who do I call?"

Doc pulls out his phone. "I'll send you the bios and contact info for the two top fae cardiologists in the country. I know the first one and can vouch for him. Neither are close by. And both are heavily sought after. It might take weeks before we can get them to her."

My phone buzzes and I scan the information the bear sent. "Consider it done. And it won't take weeks. I'll send in an extraction team in full tactical gear if necessary. One of these men will be here by tonight."

Calli

"What is *that?*" I stop as we reach the main entrance to the Prime Palace and point at a shimmering curtain hanging inside and to the left of the wall of glass doors. It glistens like watery prisms caught in full sun, hovering like a magical sheet undulating in a soft breeze. People are walking into it and out of it, yet not appearing on the opposite side.

"It's a portal door," Nakotah says, diverting our path to give the magical portal a wide berth and heading off into a corridor laden in ivory and gold. "When members of the Fae Council or other race alphas and dignitaries need an audience with my father or one of his advisors, portal doors allow them to get here more efficiently than traditional transit."

"Weren't they all closed?" I ask, confused. "Jaxx told me the history of StoneHaven and thought I was reborn as a phoenix to reopen the portal door and secure it from members of Darkside."

"This isn't a portal door to the fae realm. It's a shortcut from other places around this world to get here."

"Why didn't we take the shortcut?"

Nakotah smiles, a poignant look on his face. "I invested a great deal of my childhood into inventing ways to get out of this palace. Getting here more quickly to face what Mother says awaits, held no interest."

He shrugs me closer to his side and presses his lips to my temple. I feel more than hear the low rumble of his wolf calling out to me. "Besides, the time spent on our journey was far more important than the destination."

I study my wolf. From the wisdom in those deep chestnut eyes to his high, perfectly aligned chiseled cheekbones to his regal, straight-backed posture.

He is a nobleman. It's crazy I didn't see it before.

We take the grand tour through long passages of plush rugs, dangling candelabras, and staff in stiffly pressed uniforms. We cut across the polished floor of the grand ballroom, around the twenty-foot mahogany table in the private royal dining room, and into a kitchen that blows my mind.

It's bigger and more elaborately decked out than the kitchen of the Beverly Wilshire, a Four Seasons hotel I worked at when I was twenty-three. Kotah leads me through the aisles between stainless-steel counters, and past a wall of ovens, and butcher blocks, and kitchen staff bustling away.

I'm struck by the contrast of olfactory chaos next to auditory silence. None of the white-coats speak while they work. It's the most repressed circus I've ever seen.

"Are we raiding the fridge?" I ask, not sure why we ended up here.

"Partly," he says, opening one of the refrigerator doors on the back wall and looking to me. "Coconut cream pie?"

I nod. "I'm good with that."

He tips his head toward a bin with cutlery and I swipe us a knife and a couple of forks. "Grab three… and some plates."

"Okeydokey," I follow his request, and then we make our escape. Out the corner of my eye, I catch someone moving in to investigate. His OMG moment of recognition is hilarious. He does a double-take, stops dead, and makes a hasty retreat.

"Ready?" Kotah asks, oblivious to the eyes on him.

"Yep. Lead the way."

With our contraband in hand, we exit the kitchen out the back, weave through a warren of serious-looking staff, and push open a door to end up in a contained courtyard. It's lush and green with grapevines hanging from above and herbs and peppers growing in tidy rows.

It speaks to Kotah's character that instead of drawing attention to the royalty of the palace, he ignores the ruby-red Orientals and the gold wall sconces and rushes me straight to the kitchen garden.

As we round a raspberry bush, I spot a little wooden hut and the silhouette of someone resting out of the reach of the rays of the noon sun. Kotah tugs his shirt down, smooths a hand over his hair, and raises his knuckles.

The knock is quiet. The response he gets in return is not.

"Why knock in your palace?" barks the woman in the shadows. "Get your furry tail in here and let me see you."

"Yes ma'am." Kotah sets the pie on the little café table near the entrance and shuffles into the hut like his ass is on fire. With me still standing in the mid-day sun, my eyes can't focus on the two of them well enough to see who he's talking to. "I thought I might surprise you this time, Adahy."

"Oh, sunshine, I'm too old and have seen too much to ever be surprised."

"Maybe this then." Kotah ducks out of the shadows and extends a hand to me. His expression is more relaxed than I've ever seen. "Adahy, I want you to be the first to meet my mate. Calli is the phoenix everyone has surely been gossiping about and I was chosen as one of her guardians."

I set the plates and cutlery down and duck inside to meet— "Oh, my..." Adahy is a lady-sized raccoon wearing a laced bodice and green, leather pants with a hole at the back for her bushy, ringed tail. I blink and try not to stare. A heads up on this one might've been nice.

"It's so nice to meet you," I say, trying and failing to push down my startle.

The raccoon lady stares at me for a moment and then bursts out laughing. After a good belly laugh, she rubs her bandit mask with black, leathery fingers. "Oh, child, I appreciate the effort but yes, I'm a giant raccoon."

Kotah blushes. "My apologies to you both. I forget... To me, you're simply you."

I sigh heavily and fall further in love with my wolf.

He looks to me next. "Forgive me. I never meant to embarrass either of you. Adahy was one of my royal weapons masters while I grew up at the Northwood property."

"Just one of?"

He pushes his glasses up the bridge of his nose and offers her a sweet smile. "My apologies. She was my absolute favorite, most skilled weapons master of all time, hands-down."

"Much better."

He chuckles. "She was cursed during a raid, protecting my sister and me from a group of Darkside mages sent to abduct us. The spell merged her female form and her wildling side into one bodily state. It was irreversible."

"I'm sorry," I say. "But thank you for your sacrifice. Kotah is a male definitely worth a valiant rescue."

The lady raccoon squeezes Kotah's arm and I don't need his omega gift of empathic healing to sense the love they share. "It was and is my greatest honor to watch over him."

"I'm relieved he had someone who recognized how special he is."

Adahy steps further into the sunlight and I take in the full wonderment of her animal form. She smiles and reaches toward me, offering her small, leathery hand. "And now, there is more than one of us. The pertinent question is, phoenix, are you prepared for the battles to come? What will you sacrifice for him and all of fae kind?"

CHAPTER FIVE

Jaxx

I leave Hawk to make the arrangements for a heart specialist for Calli and find a nook inside the palace entrance where I close my eyes. Accessing the mating bond connecting the five of us gets easier every day. At first, I thought sex strengthened the weave of the tether. Then, I thought my mating crystal did it. I now think it's all emotional exchanges and meaningful interactions.

Yesterday, my connection to Calli was strongest by far, followed by Brant, Nakotah, and then far more distantly, Hawk. Today, Calli and Kotah are equal and very accessible, followed by Brant, and still trailing behind... Hawk.

As much as the avian pushes my buttons, I regret that. Fae magic recognizes us as perfect mate compliments. Not solely Calli and him, but Kotah, Brant, and me too.

I think about that bullshit he spouted the other night about his guardianship offering him a political advantage and I want to throat-punch him. He needs to get out of his way and see what we can be.

I let my instincts fire, expecting to find the other three together taking the grand tour. No. Kotah and Calli are halfway across the palace and the bear is on his own, off to my right.

I set off, tracking him down.

I'll bet my left nut Brant is in the administration offices, searching fae records. A twinge of guilt twists my guts. Hawk isn't the easiest mate, but Brant's conviction that he's the Black Knight, a duplicitous traitor to fae laws, doesn't sit right.

Even after Hawk shredded her, Calli asked us to give him a break and try. I understand he did it to save my life and I want to honor her request and not burn any bridges. Hawk is one of our quint, whether he admits it or not. He may dig his heels in but Calli is his match and will wear him down.

If Brant and I make an enemy of him, what then?

I explore the palace following the mating bond like Hansel following breadcrumbs to Gretel—an extremely hairy, muscular Gretel.

"Howdy, Bear," I say, finding Brant buried in boxes in a file storage room. "Having fun?"

"Shit-tons."

"Having any luck?"

"Nope... or maybe yes... I'm not sure how to answer that."

I grab a chair, flip it around, and straddle it.

"I wasn't able to get into the birth registration room," he says, scowling and waving a finger toward the door. "The biddy in charge is a tight-assed stickler about who gets a peek at the files, so that's a no-go until I convince a certain sweet young prince to grant us access."

"What's the yes?"

"I found the registration records and files for the three families involved. Only there's no record of the kids I know they had. The electronic system is wiped, and it's the same thing in the powers registry too. They're gone too."

"Frickety-frack."

"Yep, that sums it up."

"Is there any way to find out how many kids this might involve or who's pullin' the strings?"

Brant's jaw tightens. "We know who's pulling the strings. We're practically in bed with the puppeteer."

"You're makin' assumptions. If you're serious about the FCO investigations unit, don't you think you should base your conclusions on facts?"

"Jaguar, seriously, the guy gets off on moving all his little pawns around. Of course he'd call himself the Black Knight."

"What's in it for him? He's already rich and powerful and runs the show for almost all fae events. Why amass guns and gifted kids to make warriors? Who's he fixin' to fight?"

"What if he's part of Darkside and wants the portal open? Or doesn't want it open? I saw him spellcasting. Do you know any other wildlings with mage abilities?"

No. I don't, but that doesn't mean he's the enemy. "Maybe it's hereditary. We know nothing about his family."

Brant flips a few pages back into place. "I've been working on that too."

"You're snooping into his background and life?"

He laughs. "So, what? He snooped into ours first. Face it, Hawk's got a God complex a mile wide, and can't face the idea of not being the one in control."

All true, but I'm not convinced that makes him fae's enemy number one. "I'm just sayin'. I think it's hypocritical to judge the male for using his power and influence to further his agenda when we've benefitted from it more than once this week. It doesn't feel right to expect him to handle everything and then plot against him."

Brant scowls. "That's different. Asking him to bring in a cardiologist is about—"

I raise my hand and stop him from speaking her name. We

can't let it get out that our phoenix savior might have a heart condition.

He scowls, looking around the empty file room like he doesn't understand my interruption.

"Discretion, Bear. If it becomes known there might be a problem, it will embolden the enemy and weaken those looking to us for hope."

Brant gathers the folders he laid out and files them back into place in their boxes. "She's gonna be pissed we went behind her back to get her checked out."

"I considered that. Maybe we say she needs to have a physical to ensure her transition is progressing properly. Or maybe we all get examined and say it's a quint thing. You know, getting a baseline at the beginning to gauge how we change and grow over time."

Brant nods. "I like that. And if we all get tested, we might learn how Hawk can command physical magic."

Yeah, that blows my mind. "Just tread lightly, that's all I'm sayin'. If you're wrong about Hawk's involvement and he accepts his part in the quint, we have to live with the fallout of our actions for centuries."

"I'm not wrong."

"Good then. I'm relieved you're keepin' an open mind."

Kotah

"You're here!" Keyla knows better than to shout in the public halls of the palace, but the excitement in her voice climbs well over what our parents consider an acceptable level. Her long, brown tresses flutter back from her shoulders as she closes the distance between us. Bright blue silk trousers sway around her legs with each step and the intricately embroidered neckline of her ivory blouse dips toward the rounds of cleavage.

My sister has matured a great deal since last I saw her.

"By the Powers, big brother, you are a sight to warm my heart. I've missed you." She rushes forward, her hands extended, her eyes sparkling.

"I missed you, as well." I accept both her hands in mine, squeeze, then bow to press a kiss on her knuckles. "You are as radiant as always Keyla. Mother told me about Father. Where is he?"

She blinks. "It's the middle of the day. He's in the receiving room granting audiences. Have you been gone so long you forgot how this palace runs?"

"But Mother…" No. She wouldn't lie to me about this, would she? To further her agenda, of course she would. "Is Father truly ill or have I been misled?"

Keyla frowns. "Oh, he's certainly not well. That wouldn't stop him from performing his duties. You know what he always says about duty and honor."

I do. "A leader must embrace his duty—despite personal sentiment, obstacles, dangers, or pressures from others. To fail in this is to lose the honor of being a male of worth."

"Good. You didn't forget everything."

How could I? The lessons I learned here are burned into my very marrow. "And have you kept well in the days since I saw you last?"

Her smile slides away from me to fall on Calli. "Not as well as you, it seems. Do my senses deceive me, or have you marked this creature as your own?"

I step close to Calli's side and wrap a possessive arm around her back. "Keyla, this is Calliope Tannis, my mate."

Keyla shoots Calli with an assessing squint that would make Lady Hacey, our schoolmarm tutor proud. "I overheard Mother say she's a common-folk human, but I sense magic. What is she?"

I swallow my disappointment. It's not Keyla's fault that my mother is so unflattering. It is, however, within her power to handle it with more grace in the face of my love.

"Does she even have fae in her bloodline?"

"*She* is standing right here," Calli says catching her attention with a little wave. "How about you talk to me if you have something to say about me."

Keyla laughs, the sound musical and infectious. "Well I see why Mother doesn't like her. She's far too forward and reaches beyond her social status."

Calli stiffens and several passersby slow to take in our conversation. "I've never had the urge to initiate a teenage takedown before," Calli says, "but slapping a debutante silly is sparking all kinds of creative ideas. Lucky for you, I think too much of Kotah, and he thinks too much of you, for me to go with my first instinct."

I offer Calli an apologetic smile. "Please excuse my sister, *Chigua*. Keyla was raised to believe she stands above all others. No one has yet to knock her off that pedestal."

"I'm up for the task," Calli says, her grin forced. "I volunteer as tribute."

I squeeze her hip and secure a stronger hold. "Living a life of indulgence has taught Keyla little of the realm she represents or how to interact with its members. She's a work in progress but believe me when I say she is worth the effort."

Keyla arches a perfectly manicured brow but remains otherwise unaffected by my censure. "Wait until I tell Mother you mated her." She draws a deep breath, testing the air, and shakes her head. "A last-minute attempt to lock the cogs of your destiny, judging by the freshness of it. Well played, brother. Mother and Father will be furious."

I remind myself that I both love and have missed my sister.

"Firstly, Keyla, you will say *nothing* to Mother. My mating is my business and I will handle it. Secondly, mating Calli was not an adolescent stunt to throw in our parents' faces. I love her. You will accept that and treat her with the respect I know you are capable of if you try. Lastly, my destiny is *mine* to determine. Whether it's as the Fae Prime or a Guardian of the Phoenix or a traveling bard playing guitar and living hand to mouth, the choice is mine."

Keyla's eyes widen as she glances at the nosy crowd of onlookers now openly eavesdropping on our family squabble.

I despise palace life. "Back to your business," I snap, glaring at our audience. When they scatter, I scrub a hand over my jaw and exhale. This will be reported straight back to Mother.

I don't have much time to diffuse this bomb.

I take Calli's hand and lean close to my sister to whisper straight into her ear. "Not a word, Keyla. I mean it. If you ever wish for me to speak to you again, you will allow *me* the courtesy of handling my own affairs."

Hawk

I emerge from the shower, freshly shaven, and wrap a towel around my hips. The four-bedroom Timber Trail suite assigned to us has a five-piece bathroom behind the back wall of the living room with two bedrooms on opposite sides. Lukas and Brant's doctor friend each have private rooms across the hall. It suits our needs and honestly, Calli isn't hard to please when it comes to housing, clothing, food, or... much of anything.

I brush my teeth, thinking about how rare that is.

The memory of Kotah gifting her with the mate bracelet he made is a prime example. No gemstones. No platinum or gold.

Yet that simple leather-crafted weave with little wooden figurines carved to represent the five of us captured her heart.

When he gave it to her, she gushed and said she'd never take it off. It sounded like placation to me. Since then, I've seen her smile at that bracelet a dozen times. In the quiet moments, when she doesn't realize anyone is watching, she caresses that gift like a precious lover.

I'm man enough to admit I don't understand her—at least admit it to myself. Growing up with nothing made me determined to have only the finest things in life.

Similar situations made her grateful for every kindness.

I accused her of not learning from her situation to grow into the woman she had the potential to be. Rethinking that, I wonder if it is me who missed the mark.

"Sir?" Lukas says on the other side of the door. "It's all arranged."

I finish with the rinse and spit, and head out to the common area to hear what he has to say. He's standing behind one of the leather sofas opposite the piano, his hands clasped at his back. I sniff the air and listen. It seems we still have the suite to ourselves, so we can speak freely.

"Go ahead. What do we know?"

"The mobile medical unit will park in hanger eight on the north side of the airstrip when it arrives. Sunset is expected at 8:44 this evening and your plane will arrive after nine and taxi straight inside. Dr. Glask and his technician have both signed the non-disclosure agreement and understand what's expected of them."

Good. "And the passenger information listed on the flight manifest?"

"The pilot is named, and the two passengers are noted simply as fae dignitaries. Our man at the tower assures me that it's not uncommon to keep names off the documents when dealing with the rich and powerful."

"Excellent, Lukas. Thank you—"

The door swishes open and my attention slams back to the fact that I am standing in the center of our living quarters wearing only a towel. Damn.

If I wasn't running completely on empty, I wouldn't have made the error of being naked anywhere near Calli. Thankfully, with the question of her suffering from a possible heart condition unanswered, my libido has no intention of taking over. Calli's health far outweighs my sexual need.

"Raar. Honey, I'm home," Calli says, waggling her brows. "Yes, this is how my men will greet me upon my return from now on. Point to you Sir Barron for starting us off. Write that down, Lukas. The phoenix has spoken."

I roll my eyes and clamp my hand over the tuck of my towel to ensure it remains secure. "Lukas, you're dismissed to take care of the things we've discussed."

He fights to straighten his smirk and sobers. "Yes, sir."

When Lukas leaves, I eye the bedroom where I set my bag and hung my clothes. "If you two will excuse me, I'll get dressed. Then you can tell me about your night at the honky-tonk bar and what's kept you busy the past couple of hours."

"Hawk, wait," Kotah holds up a hand. "I have a family matter to address. May I leave Calli in your company for the next hour or so?"

Fuck. Until we know why Calli collapsed, she shouldn't be alone. I nod to make it clear I got the message. "The two of us can survive that long without killing one another, can't we, Spitfire?"

The wolf practically bolts out the door.

"Trouble on the home front?" I ask.

Calli takes a meandering stroll around the room and drags her fingers across the polished surface of the mahogany desk inside the door. "We had a slightly heated, not-so-private conversation with his sister. He wants to get to his mother before someone spills the beans about him mating me."

Right. My breath tightens in my chest. Refusing to succumb to the madness of mating heat, I lift my chin and force my hawk's fury deep down to fester in my guts. "If you'll excuse me, I need to put some clothes on."

"Don't rush on my account."

I refuse the bait. "Pour yourself a glass of wine if you like. There is also an assortment of cold meat and cheese trays in the refrigerator if you're hungry."

I slip into the bedroom, swing the door, and grab a pair of jogging pants out of my bag. I'm stepping into the first pant leg when I realize the door didn't click shut behind me.

Yep, she's leaning on the doorframe getting an eyeful. Shit. Her hunger for me is a serious aphrodisiac. It sends a lightning strike straight into my cock and there is no hiding the result. "Boundaries, Miss Tannis? Ever heard of them?"

She smiles unrepentant. "Why are you in such a hurry to put that away? It is intended for me, isn't it?"

I stomp my second foot into my pants and pull them up my thighs. "I would think that after having Kotah last night and both he and Jaxx this morning, your sex drive might be ready to gear down for a few hours."

"Touchy."

I dig in my duffle and come out with a black shirt. "Do you blame me? Should I rejoice that first Jaxx and now Kotah has altered your scent with their claim on you? Should I celebrate that when we walk through a crowd, everyone recognizes them as your mates but not me?"

Her expression softens. "I'm sorry, Hawk. I didn't realize it would bother you."

I give her my back, unable to face the compassion in her expression. "It doesn't. Not really. My hawk might be vexed but I realize I don't care. It's a trick of the mating."

"Which you want nothing to do with."

I shove my arms into the sleeveless cotton tank and force it over my head. "Exactly."

"So, the fact that you haven't slept in a week is…"

"An annoying side effect of me asserting my independence. I decide who and what I want out of my life."

She chuckles and the sound is a one-two punch to my groin. "How did it go again… Your wants became irrelevant the moment I resurrected on the side of that road. Welcome to your second chance at life. Time to get with the program."

"Using my own words against me. Well played, Spitfire. Point to you."

"Hawk, look at me." Her voice is soft, and much too calm. My body sways to obey. I close my eyes and suck in a deep breath. My resolve to resist her is weakening.

Still, I can oblige her request without succumbing to mindless passions.

When our eyes lock, the empathy swirling in her gaze nails me hard. The sex is making her more confident in her new body. Her emerald eyes blaze, and a ring of flames licks around the round of her irises. The phoenix is becoming more integrated with the woman. It's sexy as fuck.

My heart pounds, pushing my pulse up the base of my throat. The longer she stares, the more intense my need for her gets. It's a blow to my ego, but I have to drop my gaze.

If I wasn't exhausted, I wouldn't be so drawn into this. "Calli, don't. I'm too tired to fight and I don't want this."

She closes the door and shuts off the light. The blinds are closed but still leave enough light to see perfectly. "I see that you're tired. And two nights ago, when you kissed me, I felt your hawk recede and leave you in peace."

She reaches to move my duffle from the bed, but I snatch it and hold it between us. A leather satchel is a ridiculous excuse for a defensive shield, but I'm at the end of my tether and it has to do.

"Hawk, put that down and lay with me."

"I'm afraid you've got the roles reversed, Spitfire. *I* am the Dominant. I give the orders."

"No. *You* are the zombie about to collapse. Lie down."

Her questioning my lethal abilities sparks my guardian fire like a hammer to anvil. "Says the female who *did* collapse only hours ago."

Her eyes narrow. "Told you about that, did they?"

"Your guardians don't agree on much, but we all want you safe. I think it's you who needs to lie down, and maybe, for a change, not have someone sex you up."

Calli laughs. "All right, Mr. Crankypants, a compromise. Both of us lie down and no one gets sexed up. Like it or not, my presence eases the pull on your mating heat. Get some sleep. Then, when you're feeling more yourself, you can report back to the other members of the Calli Worry Club and assure them that I'm rested and well."

She tugs at the bag pressed between us and smiles. "Trust me. It's only a nap I'm after. When I seduce you, I want you well-rested and willing."

Now it's my turn to laugh. "You can't handle it, Spitfire. This morning with the others proved me right."

Her confident smile loses its sass and I regret the jab. Does she really want the kind of sex I offer? She stares at me for a few seconds longer and then deflates. "Whatever. You do you, tough guy."

I drop the bag and catch her wrist as she retreats toward the door. "I warned you, Calli. I'm not a hearts and flowers sort of male. My interactions with women outside of a professional scope are very singular."

"Yes, bathing in beautiful, educated, elegant women, I remember."

"I apologized for saying the things I said."

"Yes, you did and we're past that."

"Yet my words never seem to die their last death."

"I'm sorry. That's not fair. I'll do better."

I don't understand why I suddenly care, but I hate the disappointment flaring in her eyes. "Fine. Get in the bed. Keep your clothes on. I'm not fucking you no matter what you have in mind."

"Aw, there's my silver-tongued devil." There's no trace of her being offended in her tone or the air. In fact, the rawness of her need to protect me confuses the hell out of me.

Why does she come back for more? Why does she care?

Calli slides under the comforter. When her head hits the pillow, her hair cascades out like a shimmering, gold fan. My muscles lock in place. Can I lie with her and just *lie* with her?

I focus on the fact that she passed out this morning.

Neither my hawk nor I will endanger her life. Sex is off the table. I'll rest with her and then we'll see what Dr. Glask says tonight.

"Relax, Barron. I don't bite... well, I do, but I won't."

I roll my eyes and climb on top of the comforter. "This is a terrible idea."

CHAPTER SIX

Kotah

*T*he royal residence hasn't changed in twenty generations. It's long been the home of kings from all species, dryad, goblin, troll, elf, nymphs, satyrs, and currently wildling. None of the diminutive races have ever reigned, but it's hard to imagine a race of enraged mountain orcs obeying the commands of a pixie king. That actually would be funny to see.

And even though my father has been king all my life, and Mother has split her time between raising us in the forests of the Northwood lands and being here, I wasn't forced to live here until after puberty.

Father thought it undignified to have children underfoot who'd yet to learn how to control shifting to wolf or who were unable to flash clothes on if something unexpected happened.

It worked well for me. It meant Keyla and I grew up in the forests of North Dakota, largely unattended, and learned a love of the land we could never have gleaned from a life of living in a palace.

Father and Mother are far too long out of the trees. They lost their animal souls somewhere along the way and I will never let that happen to Keyla or me.

Inside the door, I stop and slip on the fabric booties Mother insists we wear within the residence. They are ridiculous and I despise them, but honestly, today is about picking my battles and I'm not going to start on the wrong foot—or foot*wear*.

"He *what? When?* I saw him the night before last."

My heart sinks and I curse inwardly. I close my eyes and draw a deep breath. I hate gossips. The palace is filled with a hundred people more interested in what is happening in other peoples' lives instead of worrying about their own.

Girding myself for the fight to come, I lift my chin and make my way toward Mother's private receiving room.

Raven sits at her desk in the anteroom, as always, and offers an apologetic smile when she sees me. She's a pretty lady in her mid-forties and has been Mother's right hand in running the household since before I was born. "Go right in. I believe she's eager to speak with you."

"I expect she is." I stare at the door for a moment, trying to slow my heart rate, and then I open my way and stride inside exuding far more confidence than I feel.

"Keyla, I'm disappointed in you," I say, holding a hand over my heart. My sister is perched on the corner of Mother's desk while my mother paces behind the floral settee sofa. "I told you I wanted to tell her myself."

My sister offers me a sheepish look and shrugs. "It was too much pressure to keep from Mother. You should never have asked me to lie."

Mother turns on me sour-faced. "Is that the type of behavior you learn in university, Nakotah? To coax your sister to lie to your mother about having sex with a woman you just met. Is that what my money pays for?"

I shoot Keyla a daggered glare and shake my head. "I never

asked her to lie. I simply asked that she keep her gossipy mouth shut—"

"Nakotah!"

I draw a deep breath and unclench my fists. "Apologies. I asked my dear, sweet sister to keep the news of my mating to herself for half-an-hour so I could come to tell you myself."

"And what would you have told me that differs from Keyla's account? Did you mate with that human?"

"Calli and I mated, yes, but you know she's not human. She's the reborn phoenix and it can't be a surprise to you that I mated her. I was chosen as her guardian."

Mother doesn't look at all appeased. "I thought you to have more sense. Your destiny was chiseled in granite since the day of your birth. You are to be Fae Prime after your father no longer sits as leader of our people."

"Well, now the universe has chosen a new destiny for me. Darkside is actively plotting. Calli was reborn and needs her mates to train her and ready her for the battles to come."

Mother shakes her head. "And you'll throw away your family honor and duty to serve the fae realm to play house with a common nary? Kotah, I have never been so disappointed in you. I thought the honor of you being named a Guardian of the Phoenix would make your father proud, but you were never supposed to accept it."

I bite my lip. "Being with Calli and the others is what I want, Mother. I hoped you might support my decision and respect me as an adult who knows what he wants."

Mother flings her hand in the air, dismissing that. "Respect you as an adult? Perhaps my information is faulty, but were you or were you not involved in a drunken altercation at a roadside bar less than twenty-four hours ago? Is that the act of a respectable, grown male of your standing?"

I curse inwardly. The Prima and her spies. I forgot how much I hate being under her constant watch. "And did your informant explain that I was neither drunk nor the instigator of that altercation? In fact, I stopped the altercation from coming to blows while defending a female? There's no reason for you to judge me because of that. It was nothing."

Her eyes tighten and her glare locks in. "You naïve little boy. You are the heir to the fae crown. Everything that happens with you reflects on your father and I and our place as leaders. People must have faith in your character as future Fae Prime."

She'll never listen. She'll never choose me. "I'm a Guardian of the Phoenix. That is the duty I choose."

"Fae Prime is your duty and as the highest position in our world, it supersedes all other commitments. As such, I've spoken to the Fae Council. They are looking into how to sever your bond as we speak."

"You have *no* right—"

"Nakotah Northwood, be *silent!*" She stalks in front of me, her eyes flashing with a rage I've rarely seen. "You will forget this phoenix non-sense and commit to the true problem at hand. The Fae Prime is ailing, and you must assume your role as his successor immediately."

Calli

I wake with a jolt, unsure of what's happening. It feels like a truck is parked on my chest and a harsh voice is gasping vile, angry threats into my ear. I struggle to get my brain to catch up with the panic gripping me.

My scream is caught by the hand clamping hard over my mouth. It presses down hard, forcing my head deeper into the pillow. Right. Pillow. Napping with Hawk.

Blinking madly, I try to focus.

Hawk is on top of me, glaring... but the man behind those

cold gray eyes isn't him. And whoever he's seeing isn't me. I grab at him, struggling to get free.

His chest is heaving with the effort of holding me down. "I'll fucking kill you," he growls, shifting his hand from my mouth to my throat.

My intake of air is blocked and the rush of blood in my ears is deafening. If I don't get free, he'll kill me. My phoenix ignites beneath my skin and I smell the burning of his flesh.

"Hawk," I gasp. "Please..."

The pressure of my pulse behind my eyes is intense and my vision is going spotty. My skin is aglow, and the sheets are smoldering. Panicked, I buck upward with all my strength. His hold on my throat lessens for a second and I scream. The sound is short-lived and cuts off a second later.

A flash of light from the doorway precedes the removal of Hawk's choking grip. I roll to the side, gasping and coughing for air. Angry male voices erupt but my hearing is still on the fritz. The world is drowned out by the thunder of adrenaline rushing in my ears.

I swipe my hair free from my face as Brant throws Hawk across the room. He hits the wall so hard, the drywall buckles and leaves the dent of his body.

"Don't," I choke, scrambling in a fit of kicks and struggles to get out of the twisted hold of burned sheets.

"Calli!" Jaxx flicks on the light and rushes toward me. "Are you okay?"

I push past Jaxx's embrace and stumble six feet across the floor. My legs feel like rubber and I fall past a growling bear to land ungracefully to cover Hawk. "Don't hurt him." My voice is thin and not my own. I swallow and wince at the burn of my throat. "Nightmare... not his fault."

Brant looks at me like I'm crazy. "He had his fucking hands wrapped around your throat. He was choking you."

The fog of Hawk's waking nightmare burns off. I watch as

confusion is replaced by dawning and replaced again by haunted horror. "Oh, fuck. No. I didn't."

His gaze locks on my throat. I still feel his fingers clasped around my trachea. No doubt his grip left marks. He's staring at me, looking lost... and disgusted.

"It's okay," I gasp. "I'm okay. You didn't mean to."

Brant grabs my shoulders and hauls me off the floor. "Calli, stop. You're delirious. We need to—"

I fight his hold but it's no use. I haven't got the strength in me to fight Brant's will. "Let me go, Bear, please."

"No," Hawk says, pulling himself up to sit on the floor. "Get her out of here and keep her away from me."

"No!" I shout.

The world spins and I'm in Brant's arms. He's carrying me away and something inside me knows if I don't fix this right now, Hawk will be lost to us.

"Brant put me down." I wriggle, but he refuses to listen. "Brant," I say with more force, trying to gain my freedom. "Put me down."

The fact that my wishes are being overwritten brings me to fury. The look in Hawk's gaze as he zips up his duffle terrifies me. He's broken. Utterly shredded. My heart breaks and I'm scared. Only this time, my fear isn't for me, it's for Hawk.

Something inside me surges forward and my need to help him overrides everything else.

"Do as I say. Bear. Put. Me. Down." The words are barely off my tongue when Brant straightens and sets me on my feet. I don't know who's voice came out of my mouth, but not only wasn't it mine, it was piss-my-pants freaky.

Brant looks weird.

Jaxx's jaw drops.

Kotah steps into the suite. He looks wrecked. I fight the urge to go to him. I have a more immediate fire to put out. I've got a Hawk to pull off the ledge.

"Don't disturb us," I say, heading back to the bedroom. "And whatever happens, Hawk doesn't leave this suite until I say so."

Hawk

I hear Calli warn off the others and can't comprehend where her head is at. What's wrong with her? Is it sadism... masochism... is she so royally fucked up she injects herself into volatile situations? Whatever the reason, the boomeranging needs to stop. I'm dangerous for her.

When she crosses the threshold of the bedroom, I hold up my hand to stop her. "Listen to them and let me walk out of here. I'm no good for you. *I* was the mistake in this mating. I just proved that quite spectacularly."

Calli closes the door and leans back against it looking as panicked on the outside as I feel on the inside. Well, panicked and wildly beautiful. Her emerald gaze burns with emotion and her hair is tousled like an 80s Guns and Roses video.

Yeah, except not tousled. Her hair got tangled during a fight for her life. I am such a fucked-up bastard. "I need you to know... I can't begin to tell you how horrified I am by what happened. I'm sorry... so, fucking sorry."

"You don't need to apologize."

"I attacked you!"

She juts her chin and frowns. "That wasn't you."

"Brant's right. You *are* delusional."

She pegs me with a glare. "No. I'm the only one of the five of us who can see things clearly. Your face was six inches from mine while you were choking me. I got an up-close and personal view of who was driving your train and it wasn't you."

"I'd never do it consciously, but it was still me. You don't know me."

"I *do*. I know you better now than I did twenty minutes ago. It takes one to know one, right? Who hurt you?"

Oh, hells no. I grab my bag off the floor. "I'm not discussing this with you."

"Yes, you are. You owe me that."

I scoff. "I'm your guardian, not your lover. I owe you my loyalty and my support in the days to come. I don't accept the mating, so I don't owe you any more than that."

"You dug into my darkest hours. I think a little quid pro quo might help. This can't be the first time that shit bubbled up. If you walk out of here and pretend you're all right, your past wins. Let me help."

I see the concern in her eyes, the affection, the complete dedication to fixing this. It doesn't help. Instead, it brings me to the edge of violence.

"Was it sexual abuse? Physical abuse? What?"

I turn my back on her, the last of my control slipping from my grasp. "Calli, I understand you're trying to help—though, for the life of me, I don't understand why—but I'm not that person anymore."

"If that were true, I wouldn't have woken up to play the starring role of a snuff film. Has it happened before with one of your ambrosia crowd?"

"No."

"So, it's *me*? What about me triggers that level of aggression in you. I know I don't hold a place of honor in your life, but damn it, Hawk—"

I turn and can't believe she's so fucking clueless. "It's not *you*. The females in my past... I never *slept* with them. I fucked them and left, or I fucked them and they left."

Her brow pinches. "You've never had anyone cuddle in for the night? Never?"

I growl. "I can't do this with you right now, Calli. You need to give me some space."

"No. You're as much a runner as you accuse me of being. We're talking this out." She crosses her arms and the position plumps up the rounds of her tits. My cock responds immediately. Fuck, I'm wearing track pants. There's no good way to hide it if I can't get away from her.

Unless. Yep.

I drop my clothes and call forward my hawk—literally and figuratively giving Calli the bird.

Jaxx

What the hell is happening? My gaze bounces from the devastation on Kotah's face to the blank nothingness on Brant's to the closed door where Calli and Hawk's fight suddenly goes dead quiet. My phone buzzes in my pocket and I check the ID. "Hey Mama, I... uh, need to call you back."

"Is everything all right, baby?"

"Nothing critical. I hate to say *drama* but yeah, gotta go."

"All right. We'll talk later. Love you all."

"You too, Mama."

I shove my phone into my jeans and get my head back in the game. Brant has his back against the door to the outer hall, his arms crossed, and is emitting a deadly bouncer vibe.

"What did I miss?" Kotah asks, looking as baffled as I feel. He waves a hand in front of Brant's zombie stare and frowns. "What's wrong with him?"

"Okay, my best guess is Hawk and Calli were napping and Hawk had a PTSD nightmare and almost choked Calli. Brant went into an overprotective mode and Calli blasted him with some kinda back the hell off command that has him enthralled. Calli ordered us to give her time with Hawk but says he's her prisoner until she paroles him. Brant's following her order."

Kotah draws a heavy breath. "What can we do?"

I shrug. "I think it's out of our hands for the moment. What about you? You came in here looking like your puppy got mushed on the freeway. What's up with you?"

Kotah tells me about his sister's betrayal and his mother's intention to have him severed from our bond. I can't imagine how deeply that would cut me. "She'll never break our bond. It was bullshit when Hawk said he wanted to look into it and it's bullshit now. The only way that I know of to get out of a magical contract is for it to be unanimously dissolved. Not gonna happen. You are ours, Wolf. If anyone from the outside world has a problem with that, too bad."

My family is the concrete in my foundation. Did none of my mates have that? It hits me then. "I know what you need."

"What?"

I pull out my phone and hit the call log. "Hey, Mama. Kotah's having a hard time. He's never had the love and support you guys gave me. Do you think you could lend an ear and give him one of your famous southern comfort Mama talks?"

"Of course, dear. Put him on."

I hold the phone out and point to one of the other bedrooms. "Trust me, on this. Untangling emotional messes is her specialty. Now that we're mates, she's your mama too. Tell her what you told me and how you feel about it. I promise, she'll patch you right back up. Oh, and she's a historian. You two might find you share interests."

Kotah looks at the offered cell like I'm throwing him under the bus. He'll see. My parents were serious when they said this mating gave them three more sons and a daughter. Our wolf is about to learn what it's like to be part of my pride.

His birth family may fail him, but he's in my family now.

Calli

Hawk shifting into his animal form brings all possibility of a heart-to-heart to a grinding halt. Stubborn ass. I stare at my majestic mate perched on the footboard of the bed and shake my head. "I get the impulse to withdraw, I do. But bottling up past darkness doesn't work indefinitely. Eventually, the bottle shatters or something leaks out around the cork and you find yourself getting punched in the face, hiding in a forest, or choking the woman sleeping next to you in bed."

He clacks his beak and shakes, ruffling his feathers.

I move to stand next to him. "You shifting isn't all bad, though. It gives me my first real chance to admire your bird up close." I snort. "Okay, that sounded rude and wasn't at all what I meant."

My cheeks are hot with embarrassment, but I wave it away. Maybe the adrenaline spikes of the day are knocking me for a loop. Life has been too weird today: fainting orgasms, raccoon ladies, almost being choked to death, and then calling lockdown so my wounded bird can't fly the coop.

"Of anyone, I understand the need to bury shit that doesn't define you and, failing that, the impulse to run. You get that, right? Don't front with me. Let that shit out."

Hawk tilts his head to the side and clacks his beak at me again. "I know. You're the bomb. You don't need anyone."

It's come up, many times, that avians aren't like other wildling races. They are loners. They are calculating and tend to be egocentric and narcissistic. Hawk comes off as an autocratic prick—and he can be—but I see past the façade he shows the world.

"Something happened in your past and you shifted into survival mode, just like I did. I found Riley and fought my way back to the collective—you chose to go it alone. There's nothing wrong with that. Just know that if you want someone in your corner, I'm here."

I reach to brush my fingers over the chestnut feathers of his head, and he snaps. The hook of his beak catches my finger and cuts through my flesh.

As I gasp, he clacks his beak and shrieks.

"Okay, fine! You pissy fucking jerk." I hiss, sucking my finger into my mouth. "I get it. You're not into me. You don't want me here. And there's nothing I can say that helps. Message received. Fuck you."

I swing the door open and crash straight into Lukas. While we've never gotten physical before, the fact that his chest is as solid as a concrete wall is no surprise.

Pushing back from him, I throw a thumb over my shoulder. "You want him. He's all yours. But I warn you, he's in a piss-poor mood."

"Isn't he always?" a woman asks.

I lean around the wall of Lukas and gander at the leggy, raven-haired beauty standing in the living room. She's dressed to impress in a red, sheath dress that slits up the side to show off mile-long legs and then clings to her hourglass figure. Coiffed hair, perfect porcelain skin, smokey eyes.

I hate her immediately.

"And you are?"

"Jayne Trenton, of the Manhattan Trentons," she says, strutting forward with a Cheshire grin and an elegant hand dangling between us.

A shrieking Hawk hurtles past my head and transforms mid-air, landing right in front of—

"Hawk's fiancé," she says, grinning. "Pleased to make your acquaintance, Calliope."

CHAPTER SEVEN

Hawk

"*F*iancé?" Calli bursts into a full fiery rage and lunges. It's only Lukas's preternatural reflexes that save me from a full-bodied takedown. He launches and plucks her out of the air. I give him credit. I've witnessed him take down armed assassins and monsters and violent members of the fae realm, but our phoenix in a rampage rivals them all. "You lying slugfucker... Is this a game to you... Does toying with me get you off...?"

"Calli, I'm not—"

Lukas loses hold of one of her arms and a wild swing sends me diving out of the way. A fireball singes my shoulder as I pull Jayne to the floor. We go down in an awkward tumble over the side chair and hit the ground hard.

"She's a maniac," Jayne snaps.

I shove her away before I wring her neck. "What did you think would happen? She's a week into her transition for fuck's sake."

I roll to my feet and grab Jayne's arm. Lukas nods and twists

Calli so we have a clear shot at the door. I make a break for it and reach for the knob—

Brant knocks me ass over end and I sail through the air. My hip meets the hardwood and I slide twenty feet. The breath expels from my lungs when I slam up against the legs of the piano. The bear growls, eyes unfocused. "You don't leave."

"Shit," Jaxx curses, rounding the sofa to grab my arm to pull me up. "Not his fault. Calli compelled him."

What? "When the hell did she develop compulsion?"

"She's a natural. You've got magic mojo, though, right? Can you release him?"

I roll to my knees and peek up from behind the sofa like a fucking groundhog in a hole. Utterly undignified.

Lukas is losing his hold. "She's heating up," he shouts. "Whatever you're planning, do it."

I curse and turn to Jaxx. "I can't unlock him with incoming fireballs aimed at my head."

"Then I'll get your girl out and you handle Calli." Jaxx chuckles, finding something in my expression funny. "And when I say handle her, I mean get your balls fried."

Jaxx rushes for the door and pulls Jayne against his side.

She struggles against his hold and flashes me a petulant glare. "What? You'd stay with her over me—"

In a fucking heartbeat. "Jaxx, go."

~

Kotah

I stop in the doorway of the bedroom, my mind struggling to catch up to the scene exploding in front of me. What did I miss this time? Here I thought the drama of the palace would be centered on me. Leave it to my mates to take the pressure off by unleashing our unique brand of crazy.

Brant paces, agitated, more bear than man. He's got Hawk in his sights and a threatening growl vibrates through the suite.

Hawk waits for Jaxx to exit with a very fancy woman and then rises from his crouch behind the sofa. "Calli, don't fry Lukas. He's trying to help."

"What can I do?" I ask.

"Keep the bear off me so I can get Calli calmed down."

I check out our enraged mate and chuckle. "Good luck."

Calli

I am betrayal. I am fury. I am fire. My sanity ignites like a Molotov cocktail and the fiery beast inside me erupts. He lied to me... let me believe... let me hope. I'm more ashamed of myself than I've ever been. Hawk and that bitch—that elegant, beautiful, confident bitch played me for a sucker. Of course, he doesn't want to be with me. Look at her. Look at me. He said as much right from the beginning.

You're nothing special Calli and you know it. Our world needs greatness right now. Hard truth time—that isn't you.

But I wanted it to be me.

And for a few days I thought it might be.

I'm not enough. The others don't see it yet but we're still in shiny new toy territory. Once the polish wears off, they'll see my flaws and failings.

Hawk is shrewder. He saw them from the start.

All the hope of building a new life drains out of me. All that's left is loss. Loss of a dream. Loss of my life. Loss of Riley. Oh, gawd, I miss her. The ache of it consumes me.

It's like a deluge of cold water douses my fire and my entire being sizzles away in a cloud of steam. I thought the push and pull between me and Hawk was a dance of dominance, a test of wills. No.

He laid it out for me, and I was too stupid to get it.

You've never been stupid a day in your life.

The familiar voice in my head signals the loss of my sanity as well. Now I'm hearing the voice of the dead. *Riley?*

Do you have any other besties talented enough to visit you through a mind-meld?

I've lost it. Marbles officially lost. *The last time I checked, you weren't Vulcan—you were dead.*

The me you knew maybe... but not this me.

I honestly don't care if I am crazy, hearing Riley's voice the moment I need her makes a trip into the cuckoo's nest worth it. *Ri, I miss you so much. I need you so much. You'll never believe how weird my life got since you died.*

She giggles and the sound is as crazy and free-spirited as ever. *She says to the voice of a dead girl floating in her noggin. I'll see your weird, girlfriend, and go all-in on bat-shit.*

Hawk

Calli is a force. She's fierce and feisty and when her phoenix is in ascension, intimidating as fuck. The yelling I understand. The fireballs I expect. But when she goes limp in Lukas's arms, I'm leveled with a rush of fear that liquifies my bowels.

Her heart. Oh, fuck, no.

I'll be the death of her. First, I almost strangle her, and then, I break her already tender heart. "Calli." I drop to the floor to catch her as she slides from Lukas's grip. She's not only unconscious... she's vacant.

As I take possession of her collapsed form, I wince at Lukas's burnt and blistering hands. The stench of smoldering flesh burns my nostrils. "Kotah, help Lukas. I have a burn kit in my bedroom… no, wait."

I place a gentle finger under Calli's chin and lift her gaze to meet mine. Big, fat tears are streaming down her cheeks. I'm such a fucking bastard. I swipe her cheek with my thumb and then brush both Lukas's wrists above the damage.

Scooping Calli off the floor, I take her back into the bedroom we shared for our nap. She's dead weight in my arms, her tears silently leaking out of her. "I'm here. I'm not going anywhere. I've got you, Spitfire."

Except my spitfire isn't here.

After propping the pillows and lying her on the bed, I sit on the edge of the mattress and smooth her hair back from her face. The golden strands stick to her clammy skin. Whether that's from her heated fury or her current state, I don't know.

The purple bruising impressions of my fingers manacle her throat for all to see. My eyes sting and I have to look away before I'm sick. Thanks to me being fucked-up, her pale skin is marred with a macabre choker.

"This is why I don't deserve precious things, Calli. I can't be trusted not to break them."

She won't look at me or can't… that scares me more.

I lean over her and move my face into her line of vision. "I'm not engaged, Calli. Wherever you are, hear me. I don't care about Jayne. I never asked her for a future and never would. She's not the one I want."

Nothing. Her vision is glassy, her tears steady.

I take her hand in mine, her skin still hot to the touch. I don't care. I need to reach her. "Damn it, Calli, look at me."

Calliope Tannis is a fighter. I know that. She gives as good as she gets. She's brutally honest. She's far too accepting. And her presence sings to my soul.

"How is she?" Kotah says, from behind me.

Broken because of me. My throat is too thick to speak.

"Let me help." He rests a soothing hand on my shoulder, and I shrug him off. I have no interest in being soothed.

"Don't," I say, turning to face him. It's too late. He's already seen too much. "Yes. The bastard avian does have feelings. Despite what you all think, I do care about her."

Kotah crawls onto the bed beside her. "You're only so guarded because you care too much. Even with all the things you excel at, you don't have the emotional skills to process what you feel for her."

Smart kid. Right. Psychology is his thing. "Can you soothe her with your gift and fix her?"

Kotah lays his head on the pillow beside her and rests his hand on her heart. "She's not broken. She's sad and ashamed and resigned to you not wanting to be with her."

"Why is it so easy for her to believe Jayne and not me? It's a lie. I'm not engaged."

"I suspect meeting your girlfriend and her saying you have another future planned put a face on all her worst fears. Her insecurities were proven right. She can't measure up to your standards."

I can't breathe. Rubbing my fist against my chest, I try to get my lungs to take in air. It doesn't work. I'm suffocating in self-hatred. "Calli, you're ten times the female Jayne is. She's my assistant and we spent a lot of time together. She joked one day that we should make it official. I've made it clear a hundred times I'm not interested."

I bring Calli's knuckles to my lips and kiss them. The scent of her heartache blended with the char of her recent meltdown twists in my guts.

Even in scorched clothes, with a nest of tangled hair, blotchy cheeks, and red-rimmed eyes, she steals my breath. "Calli, look at me and yell or cry or kiss me or hell, I'll even take another slap to the cheek, just wake up."

In any romance movie ever made, this is when the leading

lady blinks awake and falls into the arms of her hero and they kiss and know everything will turn out.

Except, I'm no hero.

Calli remains unresponsive.

"Please, Spitfire. I'm an idiot and a jackass, but don't give up on me yet. I'll turn this around. I swear."

Nothing.

I sit there, studying her vacant stare until my hawk is violent inside me. Reaching up, I gently brush her eyes closed. "Stay with her while she rests. I'm sure she'll wake up soon."

I hear my words as they hit the air and even I don't believe me. I can't sit and do nothing. Heading out to the living room, I eye Brant standing vigil at the door.

That shuffling buffalo farmer is six-foot-eight of solid muscle and there's no way I'm getting out of here to deal with Jayne. Either Calli needs to wake up or I need to work on breaking the thrall.

Movement on the sofa brings my attention to Lukas. "How are your hands."

He holds them out, turning them over and back for my inspection. The injured flesh is pink and tender but healing. In another hour, the damage should be fully healed.

Phoenix tears are astounding.

"Good. Call Jaxx and get him to bring Jayne back. In the meantime, I'll see about clearing the cobwebs out of the bear's mind."

Jaxx

When I get the text to bring Hawk's Manhattan hottie girlfriend back to the suite, I'm pretty sure the guy has a death wish. I call him, to double-check, but he says he's sure. Who am I to argue?

It's his funeral. Knowing Calli and her temper, it will be a blazing pyre that reaches the heavens.

"Why are you laughing?" the female snaps. "Nothing about this is funny."

I shrug. "Just imaginin' how things will play out, is all. With the two of them, it'll be quite a show. I guarantee it."

I reach for the door and give her a serious once over. She's drool-on-your-boots gorgeous and has that air of confidence high-powered corporate females have, but Hawk couldn't possibly pick her over Calli, could he?

Nah. The guy might be an ass, but he's a smart ass.

"A word of warning, Black Beauty, if you ever pull the rug out from under my mate again, I'll gag you, roll you up in that rug, and they'll never find the body. We clear?"

I don't wait to see her response. Honestly, I don't care.

Lukas meets us at the door, looking serious as the business end of a .45. "The compulsion is off the bear. He and the prince are in that bedroom with your mate. You should join them."

The tone of the guy's voice sends off all kinds of alarms. "Why? What's wrong? What happened?"

Hawk comes to the doorway of one of the other bedrooms. "You can discuss that privately with the others. Join them. I'll be in once I'm finished here. Jayne, if you would. This will only take a moment."

He sweeps his hand to usher his raven-haired honey into the room with him and I take my cue.

My cat launches forward, and I jog to the bedroom and let myself in. Brant and Kotah are standing by the window looking ill. Calli's on the bed looking—

"Shit. What happened?"

Hawk

As Jayne approaches the bedroom, I think better of closing myself in alone with her and step into the living room of the suite. Not that anything would happen between us—unless I give into my instincts and kill her—but optics are everything. There's no way I'll fuel the fire of Calli's heartache. Never again. "Lukas, if you'll excuse us, perhaps you can check on the arrival of our expected guest."

When Lukas heads out to the corridor, I rein in my hawk's need to claw Jayne's eyes out. "You're too smart to think that little grandstand performance would do anything but sever our relationship irrevocably, so why do it?"

Jayne's cool expression proves my gut instinct. There's more to this than rattling mine and Calli's cages. "I'm here for the Monster Rights conference, as scheduled, and came to bring you up to date on the last-minute changes. Despite you choosing to play house with that—" she waves her manicured fingers at the bedroom door and wrinkles her nose—"ill-mannered creature, we've worked too hard for the FCO to fall because you can't keep it in your pants."

"Careful, Jayne. You're dangling over a precipice as it is. The last thing you need is a push."

Amusement warms her eyes. "Empty threats aren't your style, darling. You don't know where half the skeletons are buried. Like the human's say, behind every successful man is a woman. Don't forget who that woman is."

"You think too highly of yourself," I say, cursing myself for allowing her to become so integral in my company. "I can end you with one phone call."

"And I've known that for years. You don't think I've taken precautions? It's you who needs to be careful, Hawk. I learned from the best."

She steps over to the sofa and flashes me her ass as she bends to pick up her handbag from where I tackled her earlier. Big mistake. I should've let Calli fireball her.

When she straightens, she glosses her ruby red lips and smiles. "I'm heading over to the Bastion. I've reserved the FCO cabin for us for the duration of the Monster Rights conference. If you want to keep the faith of your shareholders, I suggest you join me tomorrow, so we have a day to go over the objectives. You wouldn't want to look like an unprepared fool in front of the fae world now would you, darling?"

She blows me an air kiss and heads for the door.

My knuckles ache, my vice-grip on the piano the only thing holding me back from tearing her to shreds. I don't move until after the *click* of the door latch signals she's gone.

Motherfucking hell.

CHAPTER EIGHT

Calli

"This is ridiculous," I say for the umpteenth time. I meet Hawk's hard gaze in the rear-view mirror and frown. As hostile as he comes off, I sense a shift in him. Regret. Anger. Maybe even a budding hint of concern. "I didn't pass out. That's not what that was. I told you, Riley came to check in and do some sort of ghost-mortem of the past two weeks. I guess I just checked out while we were chatting."

"You say that like that's a real thing."

"Why not? I didn't believe in magic and wildling men and fireballs until I lived it. Isn't it within the realm of possibility that I'm right and Riley and I connect on a level you don't understand?" I look to Kotah. "Help me out here."

Kotah squeezes my thigh and tilts his head as if considering it. "While it's true, the possibility of afterlife visitation can't be ruled out in its entirety, Hawk is also right that there might be another more plausible answer."

"Like what?" I ask.

"Like a brain synapse misfire," Hawk snaps. "That's what

happens when you overstress your system and pass out twice in one day."

I want to remind him that it was him and his corporate sex partner who stressed me out but won't open that wound again. A worried Hawk is a crusty Hawk. At least he's here and engaging with me. "Well, I'm fine. You're all overreacting."

Jaxx tightens his grip on my hand where he sits to my right. "I don't know about your ghost whisperin' with your girl, but Hawk's right about the collapse. You were unconscious and unresponsive far too long. You scared us, kitten."

Kotah rubs his hand against the inside of my knee and offers me a wave of supernatural support. "Humor us, *Chigua*. If we all submit to some baseline testing now, in the future, if anything changes with our health, we'll have records to base decisions off. It'll be good for all of us."

I can't argue with that. In the past week we've dealt with being shot, stabbed, burned, drowned, and strangled. Having the starting points of our health worked out can't be a bad thing.

Brant rolls his shoulders and twists in the shotgun seat. "Plus, a few tests might shed some light on how your powers are coming in so fast. Compulsion isn't something magically gifted wildlings command after a decade—no matter how talented you are or how pissed you get, you shouldn't be able to do that in a week."

"I'm sorry, Bear. I didn't mean to—"

He waves that away. "That's not what I'm saying. There's too much we don't know about your transition and development. I know it wasn't your fault."

"No," Hawk says. "It was mine. I choked Calli, I upset her afterward, and then my assistant showed up and t-boned her with bullshit. This entire mess is on me."

Brant flashes him a sarcastic smile. "Look at you, hotshot. Pulling up your big-boy pants and taking your lumps for once.

Doesn't change the fact that yeah, you are a jackass, but at least you admit it."

"Hawk isn't at fault for his assistant's rant," Kotah says.

I tense. Even though Kotah isn't standing up for Jayne, the mention of her fires up my insides. "FYI, I hate that bitch."

Hawk frowns. "Jayne won't be a problem going forward. I put her on notice. You won't have to deal with her again."

"You should've fired her," Brant snaps. "She intentionally hurt Calli. She deserves more than a slap on the wrist."

Hawk frowns. "Trust me, I want to."

"Want to? You're the all-powerful corporate king, aren't you? Seems to me if you wanted to cut ties with your fuck-buddy, she'd be snipped and falling into the trash can where she belongs."

The angry hum that Hawk makes isn't as deeply bass and growly as Brant's bear or as raspy as Jaxx's jaguar purr, but it conveys his frustration and anger. He casts Brant a sideways glare. "What you don't understand—being a mere cog in my FCO machine—is the far-reaching ripple-effects I consider. I can't go with my gut and muscle through life as you do."

"I forgot. You're the game player. It's all about moving the mindless pawns around your board, right?"

"In a manner. I'm juggling a dozen high-priority projects and Jayne keeps all the balls in the air. She's been on my front line for years. After this afternoon, I intend to weed her out of my business, but right now, that's not an option."

I lean forward between the front seats. "And you sure it's only your business balls you're worried about her dropping?"

Hawk curses and pulls onto a small, private airstrip. "I'll say it as many times as you need to hear it. I've never held any interest in being engaged to, or sharing my life with, Jayne or any other female."

"Emphasis on female," Brant says. "Methinks thou doth protest too much."

Hawk rolls his eyes. "How old are you? Calli's had one hell of a day. Can we hold off on the schoolyard bluster?"

Brant shrugs. "At least I make her smile, flyboy. How's your courtship going? Oh right, she tried to kill you?"

I reach forward and squeeze Hawk's shoulder. "I didn't try to kill you."

"Too bad, he can't say the same," Brant says. "How's your throat, beautiful?"

I peg Brant with a glare. "Enough. We all have issues that bubble up. Hawk didn't intentionally attack me. Everyone in this truck knows that. So, enough with the dirt slinging."

"He's not altogether wrong," Hawk says, meeting my gaze in the rear-view. "And while I didn't mean to hurt you, it happened. I think a bit of distance will do us all good."

I straighten, not liking the sound of this at all. "No. Time together, working through what happened will do us good. Retreating accomplishes nothing."

"I'm not retreating," he says, slowing to park in front of an airplane hangar. "I'm chairing the discussions at the Monster Rights conference at the Bastion this week. I need tomorrow to prepare and then will be in and out of meetings for three days."

"But you'll come home at night, right?"

He turns the keys and the truck's beefy engine falls silent. "I'll be entertaining for dinners and drinks and stay in one of the on-site cabins."

"The FCO cabin on the water, isn't it?" Kotah asks.

Hawk nods. "It is, but it'll be occupied, so I'll arrange for a private one for Lukas and myself this time around."

I read between the lines and see the apology in Hawk's expression. He won't stay in the FCO company cabin because that's where Jayne will be.

I look between Kotah and Hawk as we get out of the truck and my heart pulls in both directions. I need to be here with

Kotah as he faces his father, but I also need to ensure Hawk doesn't pull away.

Kotah brushes my arm and a wave of calming energy comforts me. "If you need to be with Hawk, go, *Chigua*. Facing my parent's judgment is nothing new. If I know you're happy, I can face anything."

Hawk shakes his head and squeezes my wrist. "No. Calli stays here with the three of you. I'm a ten-minute helicopter ride away if you need me. Other than a few minutes here or there, I won't be available. Stay here for Kotah, work on your defensive training, and learn about the fae world. I'll be back before you know it."

~

Kotah

The next two days pass with little fanfare. Jaxx, Brant, Calli and I enjoy the gardens and grounds of the palace, work on some light defensive training, and await the summons from my father. He likely thinks having me wait for his attention is punishment—and in my life, prior to the guardianship, he would've been right—but I refuse to twist myself into knots wondering how to please him. I found where I belong and who I belong with. I refuse to lose that.

"Don't drop your guard, kitten," Jaxx says, pausing so I can step onto the training mat and fix Calli's form. "Protect your core at all costs. We're only using fists now, but when we use knives or swords it'll be important. A hit to the arm or leg will do damage, but body shots are far deadlier."

I shift behind Calli and reach around her sides. In a stance alignment we've practiced for the past couple of days, I adjust her elbow and bring her defensive arm back into position. I meet her gaze in the reflection of the living room mirror of our suite. With the furniture moved out of the center of the room, we have a wide-open space to work on Calli's training.

"Like this," I whisper behind her ear. "Protect my girls."

She casts me a flirtatious smile. "How about you give your girls some love? They're lonely, Wolf. They miss you."

And I miss them. Oh... boy, do I miss them.

Since having sex with Calli three days ago, my obsession with being naked with her soared from male anticipation to a mate's possessive need of wanting her every moment of the day and night. She is the sun to my universe, and I willingly agree to burn alive in her heat.

She grinds her backside against my groin and my mind blanks out. My resistance to two days of unrelenting advances is weak. As she tenses to shift and drop her form completely, I grip her hips to prevent her from turning to grope me. "Focus on your form."

"No. Let me focus on *your* form."

I tighten my grip on her hips. Being rough with her doesn't deter her at all. If anything, her arousal increases.

"*Chigua*, please."

Brant joins the fun and smiles. "No sex until we get the results back from your physical, beautiful. We agreed."

The whimpered huff she lets off is adorable. "No. You four agreed. I protested. I'm fine. If anything, you guys will kill me by ignoring my needs. C'mon boys," she says, glancing at each of us. "How about a little light play to take the edge off? Bear, you've kept me waiting long enough. Let me suck on that big cock of yours. I promise, no sex."

The bass rumble of Brant's laughter resonates in my chest. "Hawk said we'll get the results back from Dr. Glask today."

"Hawk is at the Bastion for his monster meetings. He'll never know."

I laugh. "Oh, he'll find out somehow. He's Hawk."

Brant grunts. "The point is that we ensure you're healthy.

Then we'll strip you naked and then Jaxx and Kotah can fight over who gets inside you first."

Her brow pinches. "Why not you, big guy? You're taking the back seat on us getting together. Why? Am I messing up with you somehow?"

He shakes his head, his brown hair brushing his broad, muscled shoulders. "Not a bit, I want you all to myself our first time. Call me greedy, or old-fashioned, but I want the whole deal: dinner, conversation, moonlight, and then hours of uninterrupted time to claim you."

Calli closes her eyes and the burning scent of her need pollutes the air of our private space. "That sounds wonderful."

His voice grows deeper. "And we have to pick our window because by the time the sun comes up, we'll be so sore and sated we won't be able to move for a week."

Unbidden, my body responds to the call of Calli's need. My wolf growls and I step back. Too late.

She felt my body stiffen against her backside and turns, determination flaring in her eyes. "That's it wolf. We'll keep it simple." She yanks her tank top off and throws it at me. She's so hungry.

I stare through the netting of her black lace bra and groan. Her nipples are peaked and tight, and the scent of her wanton brings my wolf howling forward. I hit the practice mat with Calli straddling my hips and pressing my shoulders to the floor.

"Mine."

Her primal claim never ceases to render me defenseless. Our lips are about to meet, the warmth of her breasts pressing against my chest.

A moment later, the warmth and weight of her are gone.

"*Noooo*," she wails.

Brant has her around the waist and carries her back into position. "New game," he says, holding up his finger to explain. "Instead of talking about sex, let's raise the stakes. Let's call this hangman strip sparring. For every fist you land, a piece of Kotah's clothing comes off. If you get him naked, you get your prize and can have your way with him."

Her eyes flare. "Yeah?"

"For reals. Anything you want. You can ride him, suck on him, have him fuck you up against the wall, in the showers, down on the mats. Lady's choice."

As much as I love being named as the prize, I'm not sure Brant should promise sexual carte blanche with Calli this hungry. She's proven herself a highly motivated female and none of us want to risk her health after the last time.

"Done deal," she says, shaking her arms loose at her sides. "Prepare to be dominated, Bear. Kotah, I'm coming for you."

She flips her ponytail behind her shoulder, raises her fists, and adjusts her stance to assume first position. Determination bursts off her like she's an MMA fighter going into the title match—oh, I see what he did.

Now Calli's more invested than ever before in her fight training. Instead of being distracted by sex, she's motivated by it. Smart bear.

"Remember to keep it simple," I say, realizing that the level of commitment Calli's exuding might bring her heart rate up to the same stress levels as sex and multiple orgasms. "Don't overexert."

Jaxx and I give the two of them space. We drop back to where we tossed the couch cushions on the floor and watch the show. The two of us lean back on our palms, side-by-side, with our legs stretched out.

"When the elder's council told us it's key for us to align as mates," Jaxx says, smiling at Brant and Calli, "I'm not sure stripping games during physical training is what they meant."

"Honestly, it's far better to how I grew up spending my time in this palace."

Jaxx laughs. "No doubt. Any word from on high?"

"No. I figure Mother painted me in such a disappointing light, he may not speak to me for a week or two."

"I'm sorry, my man," Jaxx says, leaning sideways to brush my shoulder with his. "It sucks."

Calli makes a good feint and lands a hit to Brant's side. "Whoop!" she yells. "Point to me, Wolf. Take it off."

I chuckle and pull my shirt over my head and drop it to the floor beside me. Calli and Brant go straight back to it. I've never seen her so motivated. "In truth, I'm fine being excommunicated. If I'm lucky, I'll be shunned altogether."

"It's not right," he says, his gaze filled with warmth. "You belong out in the world with us. We'll fight for you. You know that, right?"

I exhale and fall back to lie flat on the cushions. Stretching my arms behind my head, I stare up at the ceiling. "I do. Still, it's nice to hear."

Jaxx's phone buzzes at the same time as mine. We both check the incoming text from Hawk. *Tests back. No issues. Game on.*

Jaxx pulls his shirt off and tosses it next to mine. "Let's see how long it takes them to join in, shall we?" With that, he throws his leg over my hips and locks my mouth to his.

CHAPTER NINE

Jaxx

*W*ell, well. I'm not sure when things changed for me in this mating, but there's no question my needs have broadened. Kissing Kotah the other day started as a sexy show for Calli. Kissing him now is... wow, well, unexpected is one word for it, enlightening is another, erotic... Yes, Calli is our queen, but as Kotah's hands caress up and over my bare shoulders and his body relents to my advance, my yearning goes beyond sharing a mating bond to our phoenix.

I want *him.*

"Fuck, Wolf." I grip his wrists and pin them over his head. "How far into this mating do you picture us going?"

Breathless, Kotah looks up at me, his animal side wild and playful. "I'm going wherever you take this," he says. There's not one ounce of hesitation in him and thank fuck for that. "I'm all in—for Calli, you, us, or for whatever happens."

"Great answer."

I'm not sure if it's because Kotah is an omega or if it's his empathic gift or if his soul is so pure but I covet the contact.

Releasing my hold on his wrists, I rise over his hips and stare down at the cut of his abs, the rapid rise and fall of his pecs, and that gorgeous fucking tattoo that wraps around his neck. "It wasn't lip-service when I said you're a feast to my eyes. You rock everythin' I've got, Kotah."

All the stress the kid has held pent-up over the past few days seems to release. In a flurry of greedy hands, he grabs me by the ribs and pulls me over top of him. Our mouths reconnect with fierce possession. Man, I didn't realize he was so hungry for attention beyond Calli.

On a hard yank, Kotah goes for the hem of my sweats, pulls them over my ass and down my hips. My cock slips free and bounces against his groin.

I dismount long enough to do the same for him, yanking his pants inside out in the rush to get him naked. With both of us bare, I resume my place on top and let our cocks rub between us. We both groan.

We've been keyed up too long. Denied for days.

Skin-to-skin has me so fucking hot. I grind my hips forward and holy shit... it's too much. The friction of our cocks pinned between our bellies... sliding in spurts of pre-cum and mirroring the wet heat of the tongue duel waging war in our mouths... his hands, his energy, the dark spice of his yearning filling my lungs.

My cat lets off a growl and my balls go tight. I come hard, my hips jerking at the same time Kotah's head drops back. The wolf's breathing hitches, and his face contorts in a mask of pleasure as white ribbons of cum cream my cock as well.

"Fuck, yeah," I say, panting. I ride out our releases by licking my way across the inked fretwork banding his throat. His skin is salty and the mixed scents of our sex and sweat make my cat purr. "I like my mark on your skin, Wolf, but it's going other places too. You good for what comes next?"

I hold my breath, searching Kotah's wide, warm gaze for a hint that he might not be as eager to be fucked as I am to do the fucking.

"I am."

"I'm not," Calli says, above us. I roll to the side to see her and Brant and yeah, Kotah and I have made quite a mess. "What happened to no sex, puss? And if you think that counts for me while you two get off like *that* and keep me benched, forget it." Her workout clothes plop to the floor next to ours. "Brant, make sure the door is locked and if there's a do not disturb sign, hang it."

Brant's bear weighs in on that. "You're not supposed—"

I chuckle, getting reacquainted with oxygen. "Relax, Bear, she got the all-clear. That's what kicked this off. We were going to tease her."

Kotah laughs. "The teasing got away on us."

Calli lowers herself to join us, lying next to Kotah. "The only thing wrong with that is that I'm dying. You two are so damn hot together I almost lost it just watching you."

I cup Calli's mound and slip my fingers between her legs. She's hot and wet and her core throbs against my touch. "True story. You're ready to burst there, kitten. What would you like from your mates?"

She smiles and lays on her back. Dropping her knees open, the three of us get a glorious view of her glistening pussy. "You didn't seem finished marking Kotah. Don't let me interrupt. I'll take what I can get. Got any ideas, alpha kitty?"

My purr rolls off my chest and I know exactly what I want. Swiping my hand across the moisture we left on Kotah's navel, I gather the cream and smile. "Kotah, you get up close and personal with Calli's aching core with some sweet kisses. Face down, tail up. I'm going to get you prepped and primed for the main event. You game?"

You gotta love a guy who takes direction.

Kotah rolls onto his knees and nuzzles and nibbles the inside of Calli's thighs. She groans, digging her fingers deep into that glorious hair of his. Gripping tight, she positions him exactly where she wants him.

The wolf growls and it only takes the barest of touches for her to seize up. Her eyes roll back in her head and her smile is so fucking sexy. "Yes... gawd, this mating heat is wicked. And here I suffer for nothing. I told you I am perfectly healthy."

I chuckle. "We'll make you suffer a lot more before we're through with you, kitten. Except, this will be the good kind. Kotah, pop her legs over your shoulders, my man. Leverage her hips and go down on her good. Yeah, that's it."

I look over to where the bear has his hand down his pants and is working himself. "Brant, you can at least get in there and suckle her tits, can't you? Consider it foreplay to your big mating plans. We've got body parts unattended here."

Brant may have his own ideas of how he wants things to go down between the two of them on their mating night, but who could pass up those girls. Brant's clothes hit the pile and he's down on the mat in no time flat.

"Oh, gawd, yes..." Calli says arching those delicious peaks into his mouth.

With Kotah well and truly occupied suckling Calli's clit into his mouth, I caress the rounds of his tight and toned ass.

Calli

Brant slides over my chest, his bare skin cool against my heated flesh. His mouth slants over mine, kissing me slow and deep. He tastes like sin and succulence. My hands trace the banded muscles of his arms up to his unbearably broad shoulders and sink into his hair. He's been holding out on me, but Jaxx's alpha nature is in full swing and who could deny him anything when he's like this?

The kiss is scorching and I'm already coming undone with Kotah working me over with his mouth... and then Jaxx speaks. His voice is erotically husky and hits me like a Pavlovian aphrodisiac right in my throbbing core.

"Just a finger or two to start, Wolf. Let's see how good I can make this for you, shall we?"

Kotah's labors pause and he stiffens. His body tenses only for a moment, and then he groans and lays his forehead against my abdomen. As he absorbs whatever Jaxx is doing behind him, he sags against me. I'm not forgotten, though. He brushes his thumb over my hypersensitive knot and slips two fingers inside me.

"Like that, do you, sweet prince?" Jaxx's voice is choked, his turquoise gaze locking with mine over the prolapsed bodies of Brant and Kotah. "What about you, kitten. You look like you like it. How close are you?"

I swallow, my clenching muscles starting to keen and tighten inside me. "So close."

"More, Bear. Make her come hard. Calli, reach between Brant's legs. Didn't you say you want to get hold of his big cock earlier?"

I did... and I do.

I close my grip on Brant's erection and it kicks against my palm. His growls sends me careening. My pussy tightens viciously, then releases in a fiery burst of pleasure. A cry rips from my chest as my orgasm pours through me. Shattering, I arch and buck, held in place by Brant across my chest and Kotah at my waist.

It's too much... and not enough.

"Slide inside her, Kotah," Jaxx commands. "Crawl up her body and fill her greedy core."

Brant rolls back and his eyes are practically glowing gold with his bear. I hate to let go of him but Kotah pushes inside me and my world tilts.

"Yes... that."

He pushes to the depth of his pelvis and I cry out. For a late bloomer, he caught on fast. Pleasure ripples through me with every hot shove of his body into mine.

The pulsing of my orgasm doesn't ebb and end. Without warning, it doubles back and builds again. Desperate and wild, I dig my nails into his pumping hips.

"So, fucking beautiful," Brant growls beside me.

The moist *slap, slap, slap* of my bear jerking off registers. I want more of him, but I can't think... I can't breathe.

"Care to help a brother out," Jaxx says. "I need more lube, Bear. Why don't you drop that load right here?"

My eyes pop wide as Brant's head drops back and his body tightens with the strain of his release. Creamy ropes of cum spurt down on Kotah's ass and Jaxx swipes it up and slicks himself up. "Perfection. Your turn, Wolf. Brace yourself. You are about to be thoroughly claimed."

~

Hawk

With the first day of the Monster Rights discussions over, Lukas and I catch one of the limousines shuttling people back and forth from the castle to the compound. As we join the flow of traffic into the main lodge, I unlock the briefcase around my wrist and give it to Lukas. "Secure it in the safe here in the main lodge, if you would."

"Of course," he says, his gaze puzzled.

I appreciate that he doesn't ask, so I tell him. "I'm not using the safe in the FCO cabin because as you well remember, Jayne and I had a decisive parting of ways. I'd prefer not to underestimate the potential damage done if she feels inspired to retaliate."

He nods. "Of course, sir. I'll take care of it and name only you or me to claim it."

"Thank you. I'll be in the lounge when you're finished."

The lounge in the Bastion main lodge is upscale, elegant and provides plenty of dimly lit corners to have discreet conversations. Tonight, I simply want a rare Wagyu steak and a bottle of wine.

"Sir Barron," the maître d' says as I enter. "Your usual section, sir?"

"If there's an open table, yes." I follow him through the sea of seated dignitaries. This is a globally attended conference and a hundred fae leaders have come to partake in the discussions. We weave our way toward the back, and I meet the gazes of a dozen different males. I dip my chin in greeting but don't hold eye contact long enough to encourage conversation. The females sending out inquiring looks also get no response.

It seems my new status as one of the guardian's mates makes random people bold enough to approach me to ask about personal details of my life.

I have no idea why people think it's any of their business.

Even in the fae world, celebrity draws curiosity.

The females have been especially bold. Strange. As much as I hated the idea of being pulled off the market, the salacious invitations sparkling in the eyes of strangers hold no interest next to the wanton of a female determined to seduce me.

I chuckle. Who could've imagined a female like Calliope Tannis seducing me?

"Hawk," a female says from my left.

My guard comes up and I'm about to blow her off when I recognize Jaxx's mother rising from her seat. His father stands as well and offers me his hand.

"Mr. and Mrs. Stanton. It's nice to see you both again."

Jaxx's mother chuckles and rounds the table to give me a polite hug. Close to my ear she pauses. "You're mated to our son, dear. Maggie is as formal as you need to be. Mama's even better once you're comfortable."

A sickening panic twists in my guts and tries to climb my windpipe. Okay, now I understand Calli's nervous meltdown the night of the Bastion reception. I don't do parents. Never really had them. Don't understand what to do with them.

Pulling back, I swallow and project what I hope is a warm smile. "That's kind of you. If you'll excuse me," I gesture to the maître d' waiting to usher me to my table. "Have a wonderful rest of your evening."

"You too," Mr. Stanton says. "You did us proud today, son. Good on ye for taking the hard stand on the drow situation. After what happened to all y'all, Mama and I are behind you a hundred-and-ten percent. We need those rogue laws tightened."

"Now, John. Let the boy loose. He's got dinner waitin' on him and he's likely done with business for the night. You go on now, hon. Get yourself fed."

I accept the out with as much grace as I can and go.

When we arrive at a table for four near the waterfall, I shuck off my suit jacket and fold it over the seat of one of the other chairs. I sit in the chair that puts my back against the wall and, with the help of a brick half-wall to my right, blocks me from general view.

"May I get you anything to start, sir?"

I was looking forward to a glass of wine before, and even more after my visit with the Stanton's. "I'll have a bottle of Burgundy. I believe you have a few bottles of La Romanee Liger-Belair?

"We do, sir."

"Fine. I'd like it decanted at the table."

"Of course, sir." He bows and takes his leave.

With my back to the wall, I enjoy the sense of privacy for the first time in two days. I pull out my guardian phone and check for messages. Two contacts are awaiting a reply, Calli and Kotah. Curious about what our Prime Prince has to share with me, I open his first. He sent me a picture.

I tap on the image and expand it. Calli lays sleeping, with her hair disheveled and the champagne glow of sunrise warming her serene face. I've never seen her looking so at peace.

Funny, sleeping is when I feel the most vulnerable.

The accompanying text says.

Let her sleep for when she wakes, she will shake the world.

A Napoleon Bonaparte quote often misspoken. It's nice to have a scholar among us to get it right.

I take another look at Calli's image and go back to check the texts from Calli. I thumb the stream back to the first one from two nights ago when I arrived at the Bastion. She wanted to check that I settled in, that I wasn't withdrawing because of the choking horror, and that Jayne was nowhere near me beyond attending the meetings.

FYI: I hate that bitch.

I don't blame her. If one of Calli's ex-lovers sucker-punched me for shits and giggles, I'd have him killed. Quietly, of course, and the body would never be found. Her skeevy uncle crosses my mind. I don't feel an ounce of remorse, there.

He got what he deserved.

I skip over my assurance that my bed here is empty and smile at the one from last night.

How'd your prep day go? All set for tomorrow?

Ready for anything. Somehow, I wasn't ready for you.

;) Admission of weakness from Sir Barron. I'm psyched.

I chuckled at that and fell into bed last night with a smile on my face.

My server arrives with a wine cart and I pause to look up. "Are you ready for me to pour, sir?"

"Please." He turns up the decanting lantern and uncorks the bottle. After wiping the mouth of the bottle, he passes me the cork. The color is good, it's moist and intact and the aroma is heaven to my senses after a long day of tedium. "Very good."

Pouring slowly, he holds the bottle over the lantern and drains all but the sediment into a crystal decanter. "Would you like to sample or let it breathe?"

"I'll let it breathe a moment and pour myself when my guest arrives. That will be all for now."

The server bows and retreats and I am once again left to my musings. She sent me one not long ago.

Missing your acerbic scowl. No one scolded me all day.

I hit reply and wonder if she's up for some verbal sparring. I find I like our little duels of will more than I thought I would. *Do you want to be scolded, Spitfire?*

I wait... watching the screen. This sensation of playful cat and mouse is new to me and I admit, I like it.

Her reply comes. *By you... yeah baby, I think I do.*

I shake my head. She is absolutely not the female I thought her to be. *And what naughty deed shall I scold you for?*

I'll think of something.

I have no doubt. *Too vague. Raise your game. What naughty deed do you imagine getting a rise out of me?*

Everything I do or say pisses you off. It won't be hard.

Nothing will be hard until you learn to play. Think about it and get back to me. Lukas is here to have dinner. Later.

Lukas takes his seat opposite me, a foolish grin marring his usually serious demeanor.

I grab the neck of the decanter and pour us both a glass. "Why are you grinning?" I realize my brow is tight and I'm scowling. I jut my phone out to him. "Before you answer that, take my picture."

Lukas chuckles and does as he's told.

When he hands the phone back, I forward the picture to Calli. *Because you miss my acerbic scowl.*

I hit send and glance up to Lukas still grinning at me.

I roll my eyes and watch the tide of ruby liquid swirl in the bowl of my glass. "Go ahead. Get it off your chest."

Lukas takes a sip and swallows. "No need. It's as obvious as the smile on your face."

CHAPTER TEN

Kotah

*C*alli and I take advantage of having time to ourselves after Brant and Jaxx head out for their day. The two of them are working on a research project for the FCO and asked me to call down to the species registration office and award them access to the security logs pertaining to a couple of calls Brant made in the past year as an FCO Enforcer out on the west coast.

I do. The office is amenable, so poof, me and my mate are solo for French toast and strawberries.

"More whipped cream?" I ask.

She waves me off. "Nope. I'm stuffed. When and if I ever manage a full shift, I won't be able to get off the ground if I keep eating like I do."

"You'll master a full shift. Give yourself time. And as for adding to your curves. I don't think any of us mind."

"You're sweet. I swear I have never had an appetite like this before..." Her gaze widens as her panic flashes my way. "You don't think I could be pregnant, do you?"

"No. It's not that."

"You sound sure."

I smile and start cleaning up our mess. "I am sure. You're a wildling phoenix now. Our metabolisms consume thirty-seven percent more calories to run our bodies than humans do. Add to that your increased level of activity with the morning training sessions and all the sex, your body needs more food than you're accustomed to."

"Okay, good points. I only hope you're right."

I top up her juice tumbler and then return the pitcher to the refrigerator. "I am right. Aside from you not being fertile, legend states that a phoenix will only conceive if all four of her mates are involved at the time of fertilization."

She snorts. "Thank you, Dr. Spock."

I pause at the sink. "Isn't that the Vulcan man with the bad eyebrows on the television?"

She laughs harder and chokes on her pineapple juice. "No. That's Mr. Spock. Dr. Spock was a famous baby doctor."

I offer her the last two strips of bacon.

"No, seriously, I'm about to explode. You eat them." She finishes wiping the last of the syrup from her plate and takes it to the sink to rinse. "And how do you know I'm not fertile?"

I tap my nose. "You're not ovulating."

I sigh. "Okay, I get that wildlings have heightened senses but ew, a girl needs some privacy."

A knock ends that conversation and I jog over to answer the door. My grip tightens on the knob as I see who is waiting in the corridor. "Keyla, what are you doing here?"

My sister has the good sense to drop her gaze and look abashed. "I came to apologize to you and your mate. My behavior was childish and unbecoming."

Calli steps in behind me and wraps her arm around the back of my hips. "You torpedoed your brother after he asked you flat out not to. Because of that, your parents are treating him like dog shit stuck to the bottom of their glass slippers. That's on you."

Her face falls. She grips her braid and worries the plaits with her fingers. "And I apologize."

Calli shakes her head. "No. You don't get to say a few words of remorse and erase your guilt. You fanned the flames in this mess, what will you do to make it right?"

"I don't know..." Her gaze narrows and she shifts her gaze to me. "You forgive me, don't you? You know I didn't mean to cause this much trouble."

"How much trouble were you hoping for?" I ask. "I covered for you our whole life. Before we came here in our early teens, we were the best of friends. When did you lose that girl and become a selfish, judgmental..."

"Brat?" Calli says. "I think the word you're searching for is spoiled, selfish, judgmental brat."

Keyla's eyes grow glassy and for a moment I see a flash of the sister I once loved more than anyone else on the planet. I feel her sorrow. Although she's never without staff and suitors fawning over her, she's lonely.

I sigh and brush a hand down the sleeve of her silk blouse releasing a comforting touch. "Figure out how bad it is and maybe we can come up with a way to settle them down together. But I mean it, Keyla. Don't pull something like that again. I've got my own life now. If it means walking away from all of you to keep my happiness, I will."

Jaxx

"So, the reports you file after a security breach within the public eye are submitted to the district office and then compiled and sent to FCO head office to the risk assessment office. Once they determine if all the T's are crossed and the I's are dotted, head office sends an electronic copy here that is printed and filed."

"Yep." Brant's focus is completely consumed by the stack of birth registration certificates he's going through. "At least that's what's supposed to happen."

"So, either someone at the district office altered or shredded them and they never got sent, or the record of those kids was plucked from the system between there and here."

"No. Every responding enforcer gets a file notification when our cases are approved and sent on to head office. I write down the tracking number and mark it off against my records. The files definitely made it to head office."

"Frickety-frack." I scratch the back of my neck. "Okay, well, I asked my dad to run a quick data check through his department to see if those names are listed. If the kids' powers were recognized early, maybe Fae Rights flagged them."

Brant's glare is wholly piss-your-pants hostile. "I swore you to secrecy, Jaguar. Your dad using his company connections to investigate this is the opposite of conducting a low-profile search. What if whoever is behind this gets flagged if his search is detected? He might inadvertently tip our hand."

"Tip our hand to what? There's no record anywhere of anythin' you say. How do we prove there's wrongdoing if we can't even prove these kids are real?"

Brant points a finger at me. "You should've run this by me first, Jaxx. Whoever is behind this makes people disappear. Poof. Gone. If your dad mentions this to the wrong person—"

"—He won't," I say, my chest suddenly tight. "I told him to keep it quiet. He'll be discreet."

Brant gives me another ocular version of fuck you and goes back to his birth records. "Our problems are bigger than that anyway."

Awesome "Yeah? How's that?"

"Those three kids aren't the only members of fae society who were never born or registered."

"No? Who else is missing?"

"No. Not missing, just not who he says he is. There is no record of any Hawk Barron ever being born. The guy's lying and has been for years."

Fuckety-fuck. "Maybe it's a clerical error."

"Or maybe he's Darkside and is a sleeper agent rising through the ranks to topple fae diplomacy. Think about it. Is it more likely that he's a poor street kid who remade himself a billionaire or that he's got dirty money behind him? Maybe Calli and her bestie stumbled on the money venture Darkside's been using to fund Hawk's cover."

"I don't believe that. He's got his issues but—"

"What if choking Calli wasn't an accident? I was there, Jaxx. That son-of-a-bitch was full-on homicidal and crushing the breath out of her. Maybe that was another attempt on her life from Darkside."

It's a good thing I'm sitting down because that possibility makes my legs tremble. What if Brant is right? Has the universe put the male triggering the need to open the portal gate right in our lap? Has Hawk been gift-wrapped for us to stop?

"I need a drink."

"Now you're catching on," Brant quips, nodding. "Start giving my theory some merit and believe me when I say there's danger afoot. Hawk isn't who he says he is, and we need to prove it for all our sakes."

～

Calli

Kotah and I finish with our afternoon meditation and I hit the showers thinking I'm making strides in connecting with my phoenix. We made friends, as Kotah calls it, and I can call the power to the fore and ease it back with some degree of confidence. He assures me once I have command of my powers, I'll be able to explode into a fifteen-foot bird with a flaming wingspan of thirty feet. How terrifying is that?

Fresh from the shower, I towel off and pull on a pair of stretch pants and Riley's old Cal Tech sweatshirt. We found it at a thrift store when we were twenty-two and she used to wear it and pretend we lived different lives.

I stare at the mirror as I pull a brush through my wet hair. Damn it, Riley. I miss you to the depths of my battered soul.

Try as I might, no matter how meditative I get or how much I call her to me, the ghost of Riley present hasn't come back to check in.

Maybe Hawk is right, and I imagined the whole thing.

The *thump, thump, thump* on the door of the suite is a real fist-pounder, so I head out with my brush in hand to make sure someone's around to get it. Jaxx is way ahead of me and lets in Brant, Doc, and Kotah, each with their arms full.

"What's all this?" I say, rushing to help Kotah with some of the bottles he's juggling.

"It's a party in the making, beautiful," Brant says, setting his box on the counter. "We've got liquor and a blender and ice and little umbrellas and everything we need to have ourselves one helluva bash." He sets down his box and points. "Doc, set up the pong table there."

Doc carries the folding table into the center of our training space. Jaxx grabs the red solo cups from Brant's box and starts setting up.

As much as it saddens me that we're planning our first big blowout night without Hawk, there's no slowing the roll of this party bus. "Did anyone bring food?"

Kotah chuckles. "I have the food, don't worry. I won't let you or your phoenix go hungry. Adahy sent up all my favorites and some things she thought you might like as well."

All right, I say, pulling stacked trays of nourishment out of Kotah's box. "Then we can begin. Who's Mr. D.J. tonight?"

~

Hawk

"So, tomorrow at ten-thirty," Jayne says, consulting the agenda on her tablet, "the pixie queen is hosting a champagne brunch and asks you to speak to the loss of green space within large city centers. Then, you're back at the castle at one for three back-to-back sessions. At six, you deliver closing remarks, and then we all go home."

My phone vibrates against my front hip and I catch myself before I smile and fish it out. Hawk Barron, billionaire business mogul isn't pussy-whipped and missing his mate. He's cool and controlled, no matter how much of an act it is.

"Today went well, Jayne. I'll meet you in the lobby tomorrow morning at ten."

The female may have lost my faith as a companion and friend, but there is no denying she's meticulous in all manner of my business. Her entire family is made up of wealthy, powerful fae. No lackluster offspring allowed.

"Since it doesn't appear that you will be returning to the office any time soon. I need another hour of your time to go over the land contracts and a few other pressing matters which need your attention."

Another text buzzes against my hip and I curse.

Sometimes it sucks being a billionaire business mogul. "Fine. One hour, I'll get a table in the lounge."

Jayne flips her hair back. It's so black it shines blue in the ambient light of the lobby of the Bastion main lodge. "The documents are in the company cabin. It makes no sense to go there, get everything, simply to bring it back here, and have nowhere to set it out properly. You're being childish, darling."

I glare. "You no longer call me that."

She sighs, her face lined with frustration. "You're being childish, *Hawk*. You've been alone with me a million times and survived to tell the tale. Do you honestly think I'll try to seduce you or compromise you in some way?"

"In a heartbeat."

Another text comes in and I can't stand it. "Excuse me one moment," I say to Jayne stepping away.

I call up my texts and read the three missives from Calli.

Druck dialing you. Booty call.

I won pina colada pong. Suck it, Bear.

Give that beotch Jane the finger from me. The middle one.

I close my eyes and reign in my exasperation. I'm all for unwinding and sloughing off the pressures of life, but Calli is under heavy scrutiny from the fae world and the royal family and she's currently in the palace *aaaand* has had more near-death close calls in the past two weeks than I care to recount.

The four of them getting pissed drunk is not the answer.

I shuffle back to where Jayne is chatting with a dryad minister. "Excuse the interruption ladies. Jayne, I'm sorry, but something has come up. I'll see you in the morning."

Before she has a chance to rebut, I turn and collide straight into—"Damn, John, I'm sorry." I steady Jaxx's father after practically bowling him over. "I was preoccupied and not paying attention."

The jaguar smiles and it's as easy and genuine as golden boy's. "My fault, son. I wanted to speak to you privately before you rushed off. My meetings are over, and Maggie and I are heading home in the morning. Will you be speaking to Jaxx tonight?"

"I'm headed there now, yes."

107

"Good, can you let him know that the matter he asked me to investigate was as fruitless as what all y'all came up with. Those names didn't turn up anywhere in the Fae Rights database either. As much as I hate to think there is corruption in the FCO head office, I can't explain it any other way. You've got a real mystery on your hands, son."

I blink and feign a level of calm I don't feel in any way. "Yes, I sure do."

CHAPTER ELEVEN

Calli

"No, you cheat," I say, scowling at my almost naked bear with my fists poised. "That was a point and you know it. Drop 'em and give me twenty."

I point to the ground and Brant relents. He peels off the last of his clothes with a cocky grin and gives me a frontal view of a hip waggle. "I let you win."

"Bullshit." My mind goes wooly, staring at the dangling temptation of his freed cock. There are showers and there are growers. Brant is a shower. Oh, and what a show.

He stiffens and then tips like a massive oak free-falling to the floor, catching himself on his broad palms. Then the breathtaking show of his muscles flexing begins as he gives me another rep of his special military-style push-ups.

"Man, I could watch that ass dimple all night long."

Jaxx snorts at the stove and pulls out midnight nachos. "You have been watchin' it all night."

"Yes, I have." I grin and move closer. "Okay, pause, Bear. Bonus round, I'm climbing aboard."

"Are you sure that's a good idea, *Chigua*," Kotah says, stumbling over to steady me. His concern whispers through my cloud of tequila and rum and I love him for it. "You just said you don't feel well."

Did I? I gauge my buzz and though the world is spinny and my tummy is sloshy, I feel *gooood*. "Yep, I'm sure." I lean forward, brace my hands on his shoulders, and climb aboard the bear plank fun ride.

The upsy-downsy resumes, and I decide Kotah is right. My throat thickens with the urge to hurl and I dismount. It's not graceful and I hit the floor with a crash of ass, elbows, and—ouch—the back of my head.

Strong hands scoop me into the air, and I press my cheek against a crisp, silk dress-shirt. I startle and drop my head back to verify. The world blurs in a dizzying spin but yep, that harsh steel-gray scowl makes my stomach tilt-a-whirl even more.

"You *came!*" I cling to Hawk's chest and for one brief second all is right in my world—and then that brief second ends. "I'm gonna throw up."

A rush of panic churns my full belly. My pina cola margarita mash-up pushes at the back of my throat and ejects. Somehow, I'm doubled over the kitchen sink, my hands braced on the counter.

"Yes, Spitfire," he says, with quiet disapproval. "I came. And just in the nick of time, it seems."

∾

Hawk

I clasp Calli's hair away from her face as she retches her night's misadventures into the stainless-steel basin. Wearing only her bra and panties, it's easy to gauge that her skin is clammy, and her muscles are trembling with the efforts of emptying alcohol from her system. She heaves forward again and again, and my hawk's fury rages free.

"How much did she drink?"

Kotah looks at me and sobers. "She lost margarita pong but won the pina colada round."

"And we had a few lemon drop shooters," Jaxx adds, bringing over a plate of nachos.

Kotah steadies himself on the counter on her other side and places a soothing hand on her back. His touch brushes my hand and the magical energy he commands tingles into my hand and up my arm.

I shift to end the contact, in no mood to be placated.

Doc comes out of the washroom and my pique doubles. What. The. Fuck. "Party's over, Bear. You need to leave."

The male has the good sense not to argue.

Brant rises from the floor, naked and looking pissed. "Hey, he was here on my invitation. What gives you the right to barge into our party and order my friend out?"

"He's a control freak," Calli sputters, her voice echoing in the steel confines of her current position.

"Calli is scantily dressed and altered by alcohol and you invite another male to see her? What the fuck is wrong with you three? He may be your friend but he's not one of us."

"And you are?"

Brant's counter shouldn't bother me. It does. As often as I made it clear I don't want to be one of them, it pierces me through the heart to walk into their party and know I wasn't missed or wanted.

I grab a plastic cup and shift the faucet to the far edge of the sink to run the water cold. "Swish, spit, and then drink."

"So dicta...tur...torial"

"Dictatorial," I say, easing her struggle with the word. "Yes, I'm dictatorial, now do as I say."

Her submission is the only thing that keeps my fury caged.

I turn my anger on Jaxx, busily munching on tortilla chips. He's naked other than the apron tied around his waist and it hits me that my life is now some kind of a hedonistic free-for-all. "I ran into your father tonight and he mentioned the search you had him do? You're investigating corruption in the head office? What's that about and why didn't you come to me?"

The guilt that consumes the jaguar's expression says it all.

Another dagger through the heart. I nod to Kotah to take care of Calli and round the island of the kitchen to face my accuser. "You think *I'm* corrupt? You're investigating *me?*"

Jaxx shakes his head and darts a worried gaze to Brant.

I shift gears and it clicks. "No, *you* are the one vying for FCO investigations. It's you who thinks I'm dirty and you're digging around behind my back to prove it."

Brant shrugs. "What? You already admitted to investigating us. It's no different."

"Like fuck it's not. I gathered facts about your lives to pull together a composite picture of what we are as a team of five. You're on a witch hunt with a clear objective to discredit me. That's a big fucking difference."

"Okay, well if I'm so off-base let's start with who the fuck you are because no Hawk Barron was born into the fae."

I grunt and roll my eyes. "I was born Sabastian Barron Whitehouse the fifth in a small town outside of London. My family is a bunch of twisted, sadistic fucks, so I hopped on a boat at fifteen and reinvented myself. All of which, I would have told you if you asked."

Brant chuffs, advancing on me. "Bullshit, you tell us nothing. We're the grunts you're saddled with not your mates. You don't interact with us, you handle us. We're pawns in your fucking chess game, right? I bet getting mated to the guardian squad fucked up your plans."

The way he says that tweaks my last nerve. "Unbelievable, you think *I'm* the Black Knight."

Brant

At six-foot-four, the avian emanates stone-cold killer on a good day. This is obvi not one of those. His murderous intent takes him over a split-second before he bends at the waist and rushes me like a defensive tackle going after a takedown. He hits me like a tank bashing through a brick wall and the suite spins. Ass-planted and back-flatted on the floor, my face gets up close and personal with the guy's silver ring.

Fuck, Hawk has fists like Holyfield.

Heavily impaired by drink, it takes my soggy brain a bit to muster a defense. When his steel forearm pins my throat to the floor, my bear weighs in.

He may have the element of all his faculties firing, but I have strength. I grab him by his fancy shirt and toss him off me like a designer ragdoll. I roll to my feet and now it's me on top of him leading the assault. Two weeks of built-up hostility bleeds out and blood splatters the beige carpet.

"Don't fuck with me, Hawk. I've had enough of you."

I get strong-armed from behind and my bear reacts on instinct. I spin and back-fist Jaxx to the side of the head. He's thrown back and snaps the arm of the couch just as the door swings open and our regal Prima steps into the war zone.

She takes it all in and turns to glare at the kid.

Fucking hell.

Kotah

Of all the turns the night could've taken, I never saw this coming. Brant naked and spraying Hawk's blood across the décor, Jaxx sprawled out cold over the arm of a sofa with his apron flipped up around his hips, Calli dry heaving her guts out over the kitchen sink, in her lacy underthings, and my uptight judge and jury walking in at the perfect moment to take in the glory of our all-out mate brawl. I catch the flash of fury as she stares at the char marks on the wall from Calli and Hawk's fireball fight and pressure builds in my chest.

I try to push it down, but there's no stopping it. It's been building for twenty years and the pressure is too much. My mouth opens and I bust out laughing—loud, side-splitting, belly-busting roars of hilarity.

I can't help it. It's too much.

I scan the war zone and my mates and love this dysfunctional life so much more for its authenticity than all the years of royal grandeur. I love them so much.

They are my family. These hot-headed, surly, sex-driven four mismatched characters are everything I always wanted in my life and never knew could be possible.

"Hello, Mother," I manage after a long while. I wipe the tears from my eyes and find my sister standing open-mouthed behind the wall of indignance that is my mother's natural state. "Keyla, come help Calli while I greet our queen properly."

Keyla hustles around the island and her apologetic look widens when she sees that yep, I'm naked too. With a little extra swagger in my hips, I saunter out to face the firing squad. "We weren't expecting guests, or we would've tidied up."

Mother's glare is icy but doesn't touch the warmth in my soul. "You're drunk, Nakotah."

"Yes Mother, I am delightfully polluted. Thank you for finally taking notice of something about me."

Her lips pinch into a hard line. "How dare you come into this house and disrespect your father and your station with such tawdry behavior."

"How dare you think you could take these four from me. They are my home and my heart. Your back-room politics will never change that. Have the elders explained that to you yet?"

By her indignant scowl, I see they have. "Nakeyla convinced me to give you a chance to explain your mate bond and what it means to you. I see what it means. It's your way of punishing your father and me for all the perceived slights you judge us for."

I shake my head, sensing as Hawk, Brant, and Jaxx come to stand at my back. Strong and silent, they lend me strength. Calli steps into my side draped in Hawk's dress shirt. I wrap my arm around her shoulder, kiss the side of her head, and breathe her into the depths of my lungs. "Believe it or not, Mother. My guardian bonds have nothing to do with you. Fae magic chose me to serve and I accept my duty with honor."

"Well, it's too bad for you that Prime duties take precedence over being a Guardian of the Phoenix. Your father and I spoke before the Fae Council early this evening and they agree. You will serve as Fae Prime as the law dictates."

"Why me, Mother?" I say, the buzz of my night taking a sinking dip. "If you're keen on staying in power, petition the council to have the Prima take the throne until the end of the Northwood rule. There are no laws against females being in power and you already know all the players and enjoy the politics. Let me live my life. For once, choose me over what's expected."

My mother stares at me like I'm that five-year-old pup who broke her favorite crystal vase and needed a sound scolding. "You will leave the palace immediately and go north. I will make all the arrangements with Logan Silver Fox for the transfer of power and when your father's next world journey begins, by the Powers, Nakotah, you *will* return here to serve the fae. And make no mistake, you will do it with Northwood grace."

She spins and retreats, leaving no opening for argument. The door slams and sucks all the oxygen from my lungs.

Calli

It takes over an hour for seven of us to right the suite and pack our bags. Keyla turns out to be an eager helper and for the first time, I see what Kotah sees. She believed convincing their mother to give him another chance to explain would help. She just should've given us a heads-up. You never know when someone is having a naked drunken brawl and isn't receiving.

Live and learn.

In the end, Doc and Brant find some tools and get the sofa patched back together, I get most of the blood out of the carpet, and other than the scorched spots on the wall in the living room and the caved drywall in the bedroom where PTSD Hawk got flung, our little home away from home is no worse for wear.

"Thanks for your help." I offer Keyla a hug at the edge of the helipad. "We'll see you again soon."

"I'm sure," she says, her long bangs battering her face from the wind of the rotors. "And again, I hope you accept my apologies. I was wrong, but I'll do better. I love Kotah and want him to be happy. You four make him happier than I've ever seen him. You have my vote."

"Thanks."

I squeeze Kotah's hand and leave him to say his goodbyes. Hawk is waiting at the door to the helicopter and takes my bag. His jaw is solidly clenched, and he hasn't said a word since his fight with Brant. I see the hurt and disappointment he hides from the others and it breaks my heart.

Before he helps me into his sleek black and silver bird, I

squeeze his arm. "I didn't know anything about it. I would've kicked their asses and still intend to."

His chin dips. That's all I get, and I decide not to push. I accept his hand up and take one of the two captain's chairs facing the bench seat of four against the back. The plush, ivory leather creaks as I settle, and I glare at the other two sitting opposite me. "I can't believe you did that."

"I'm sorry, kitten. You have to know—"

I raise my finger and he stops. "What I know is that you two plotted behind my back and lied to my face about giving him an honest chance. Do you honestly think Hawk is the bastard behind gun-running, drow gangs, abduction of women, and the attack on my life? How far up your asses have you shoved your good sense? I expected so much more from you."

Jaxx looks stricken.

Brant, however, is the one with guilt all over his stupidly perfect face. "It's on me, beautiful—all of it. I came into this mating with a mystery to solve from my job and the deeper I dig, the more compelling my case gets toward Hawk. I'm sorry that it came out like this, but I'm not wrong."

I swallow and clasp my fingers together to keep me from doing something I may or may not regret. "Yes, you are. And once we land and I can look at you without wanting to fireball your ass, we'll talk it out and I'll prove it. Was Kotah in on it?"

They both shake their heads. *Good. That's good.*

Brant sighs. "And Jaxx has been a constant supporter for Hawk's side since I brought him in on my suspicions. If you're mad at anyone, it should be me."

"Oh, don't worry. It is."

Kotah claims the other captain's chair, Doc and Lukas buckle in on the bench, and Hawk joins the pilot up front.

Ten minutes doesn't seem like a long time, but when you're holding back a fiery beast from frying someone you care about, in a vehicle that can plummet to the farm fields below, it's freaking forever.

To allow some of the steam building in my chest time to cool, I pull out my phone and look up the deets on the helicopter. The Eurocopter AS365 Dauphin. Twin-engine. Long-range luxury transport. Seating capacity of eight. Price tag of—holy shitters—ten million. Damn. Just how rich is he?

My mind spins out on that one. No wonder he didn't want me swooping in and robbing the golden eggs out of his nest. I make a mental note to talk to Lukas about that prenup.

We jolt hard to the left and my arm cracks the wall with a bang. Pain shoots from my wrist up my arm and it's too bad my buzz canceled out once the booze ejected from my system.

No lingering anesthetic... but no hangover either.

Phoenix healing is real.

Kotah twists to check on me and we jostle the other way and then down and then we're on some stupid funhouse roller-coaster without the fun. "What's happening?"

Whatever it is, Lukas is on it. He unbuckles and launches between mine and Kotah's chairs. He's reaching into the pilot space but there's no room for another body, so his legs kick and twist as he wrestles with something over the seat partition.

We jerk left and Hawk curses. "Get him off the controls."

Who? The pilot? Shouldn't the pilot access the controls? Isn't that essential to keep us in the air? Lukas is struggling and man, I thought Hawk was bad with the cursing. Lukas strings together the most impressive run of obscenities I've ever heard.

And that's saying something.

Brant is up and reaching past me. He swings his fist, his massive size giving him one hell of a long reach. He pulls back and he's got the pilot and Lukas both.

The pilot is fighting for his life and the three of them curse and bounce around the small space. I turn away, protecting my face and try not to let the whole 'we're going to crash' reality send me into a fit of hysteria.

We jerk once more and level out, the change in pitch sending Brant charging at the far wall with the pilot in his grasp. They hit the door with the force of a tank, grappling and scrambling for purchase. Alarms sound and before my brain catches up, the door gives way and the two of them hurtle as one into darkness.

A violent head rush makes me dizzy.

He fell out of the helicopter.

Brant is gone.

CHAPTER TWELVE

Calli

"*B*rant!" I can't even... I stare at the black void beyond the door and my heart hammers at the base of my throat. My hands are trembling so bad I can't make my fingers work to release my seatbelt. Brant tackled a man out of a flying helicopter. Of all the meat-headed, stupid, heroic things he could've done.

He's got to be okay. He can't die with me mad at him. We have to make up. We haven't had our mate date.

Kotah's hands tighten on mine and I smack at the interference. "Calli, stay in your seat. Look at me. Whatever happened to Brant, it doesn't help to have you jump out after him."

Thankfully, the helicopter bumps to the ground and Lukas and Doc bolt outside. Jaxx is kneeling in front of me in the next second. He grabs both my trembling hands in his and squeezes. "Kitten, give Doc and Lukas a minute to assess the situation before you rush out there, okay?"

"No. Not okay. Brant isn't a situation, Jaxx. He's ours." My voice clogs my throat, and I can't breathe. My brain hurts and my heart aches. "I was so mad at him... He's such a stubborn... stupid..."

Hawk appears at the door and extends his arms. "Come here, Spitfire. We need you."

I'm out of my seat and running with Hawk in the next beat of my racing heart. The sirens of emergency vehicles whine in the not too distant area and I pray an ambulance is coming. Lost behind a glossy wall of tears, I have no idea where I am, only that Hawk has my hand and he's taking me to Brant.

I drop to the asphalt next to Doc and wince at the blood.

"He used the pilot as a landing pad to break the impact," Lukas says. "That saved him from the brunt of the impact."

"Oh, thank gawd."

"It's still not good," Doc says. "His wrists are broken, definitely a couple of ribs, and maybe some internal bleeding. His head looks like it took a good bounce too."

I brush my hand against his cheek, sickened by the sticky warmth drenching his neck and hair.

"There's not much I can say for sure until we get him to a hospital. You're up, Calli. Do your thing."

It's involuntary. My tears are already brimming my eyes and hot on my cheeks. As I crouch over Brant's massive frame the waterworks fall.

Kotah said me owning what happened on the side of that road means owning all of it, facing the pain of my life losses, and allowing myself to feel again. Being detached from my emotions kept me safe for a decade, but now I'm stronger.

I have a new life. I have them.

Hawk

The eastern sky is a mass of faint gray-pink swirls by the time we get back to my cabin at the FCO compound. Calli climbs out of the back of the SUV with a very wonky grizzly bear right behind her. I point her toward the second bedroom, and she and Kotah go in to get him settled. Jaxx heads straight to the bar to pour us each a drink.

When he offers it, he holds it until I meet his gaze. "I'm sorry for my part in Brant's investigation. I genuinely argued your case."

"Hoping he was wrong or knowing it?" I see the answer but accept the peace offering anyway. They don't trust me. Even after everything I've done and spent and shoved to the side to make them my priority, they still question my intentions.

I sigh and let the burn of the expensive amber slide down my throat. It's the same whiskey I drank last night, only tonight it doesn't soothe me. "I need to get through today and then we'll work on sorting all this out. You four rest here while I finish this conference. Then we'll head to Kotah's family lands and figure out the Prime issue, who's trying to kill us, Brant's mystery corruption conspiracy, the crystal hunt, and any other crisis that pops up between now and then."

"To the guardians," he says lifting his glass. "Living the dream." Jaxx tips back his tumbler and empties it on a one-gulp swallow.

I acknowledge his toast and finish mine too. "Okay. I've got four hours before I have to wake up and attend a brunch with the pixies. I'll meet you all for dinner in the lounge after six and then we'll head over to the plane."

"Are you comfortable flying so soon after tonight?"

I shrug. "Two hours in the air or twelve on the ground. Both have risks. Technically, the flight went fine. It was the pilot that tried to slam us into a hillside."

"Good on you for noticing and saving our asses."

"Despite Brant's conviction to the contrary, I'm not the

enemy here, Jaxx." I eye my bedroom door and sigh. "I'll have Lukas scrutinize the vetting of the flight crew backward and forward. We can make our final decision over dinner."

"At the risk of pissing you off, can I ask you something?"

"You're in luck. I'm too tired to get pissed."

"Are you okay with Calli sleeping here? I mean, you aren't dangerous to her, are you?"

Ouch. But I don't blame him for asking. "Dr. Glask gave me pills that will prevent a murderous encore. I'll take one before I lie down."

"Good enough. Tomorrow night then."

I head into the bathroom to clean up, pop one of the little yellow pills, and then hit the mattress without bothering to get undressed.

Calli

It's almost six a.m. by the time I'm comfortable leaving Brant's bear sawing logs next to Kotah's wolf. I find Jaxx sacked out on the couch and bypass him for the bathroom. After all the drinking and vomiting, the inside of my mouth is as foul and gritty as a litter box. I consider Hawk's comment about personal boundaries and chuckle. Then, I grab his toothbrush and do a double-the-paste routine.

After patting my face dry, I pick up the little pill bottle sitting at the top of his toiletries bag. It was prescribed the other night by Dr. Glask. What's Hawk taking and why?

The edge of the tub is cool on my butt as I sit and look it up. A sedative-hypnotic to prevent violent sleep disturbance.

I close my eyes and draw a steadying breath. How can Brant be so misguided to believe Hawk a monster? Broody. Superior. Guarded. Sure. He is a great many bristly traits but loyal, noble, and attentive are also on the list. Hawk holds the world to a code of ethics and bases his worth on how he contributes.

Why doesn't Brant see that? What makes my bear so jaded against him? It's sad. But hey, who said becoming a legendary quint would be easy?

Setting the pills back where I found them, I let myself into Hawk's room and crawl into bed. Careful not to wake him, I pull the duvet up and notice the tense line of his jaw and the pinch of his brow. Even in his sleep he looks tense and guarded.

What happened to young Sabastian Barron Whitehouse the fifth to set him on his quest of dominance and isolation? As much as he'll protest that I took liberties by inviting myself into his bed, I saw his pain back in the suite at the palace.

He needs to know I never doubted him for a second.

It takes one to know one.

Kotah

My ears twitch and I wake to a sense of being watched. My wolf senses heighten, searching for a threat. I raise my muzzle to find Hawk looking in on Brant and me from a slivered opening in the door. He meets my gaze and tilts his head toward the corridor. Dropping my front paws to the floor, I drag my hind legs on the mattress and stretch before trotting off to follow.

Shifting as I pass Jaxx sleeping on the sofa, I flash on a pair of pajama pants and follow the trail of Hawk's scent out of the cabin to the sheltered porch looking into the trees.

"Sorry to wake you," Hawk says, as I join him.

There are times when Hawk wears workout pants and a t-shirt, when he seems like an ordinary guy. Then, there are others, like now, dressed in his expensive suit with a silk, steel-gray tie that matches his eyes, that he is unmistakably as rich and powerful as the dignitaries I saw traipsing in and out of the castle for years.

I finger through my hair and shake off the last vestiges of sleep. "Not a problem. What's up?"

"First off, I want to apologize for my part in your banishment last night. My temper got the better of me and I acted like a brute in your parent's home. It guts me that you were judged based on my poor behavior."

I wave that away. "I've been judged by them my entire life. Last night, seeing Mother's jaw drop, from the chaos and depravity of our private life... that was the best memory I have of her."

"Still, it didn't help your case."

I cast a lazy glance out at the rabbit hopping along the tree line. "My father wouldn't have listened to my heart's desire anyway. Being forced into my position as Fae Prime was always their plan."

"We still have time to think of something," he says.

I hope he's as smart and powerful as I think he is. "I owe you an apology too."

"For what?"

"I vouched for Brant with the palace registration office and permitted him to access records. I didn't realize he was looking into you, but that doesn't erase my part in your pain. It wasn't right. Like Calli, I know who you are and that you belong with us. I'm sorry he implied otherwise."

His smile is forced and doesn't reach his eyes. "Speaking of Calli, I want you to stick close to her today and stay in the cabin. Two overt attempts on her life are two too many. The fewer the people who know she's here, the better."

He lifts his watch and frowns. "Shit, I've got to go. If you have half a brain, you don't piss off the pixie queen. She's tiny but she's mean."

I chuckle. "Go. We'll take every precaution."

"I assigned Lukas and a team to shadow you all today. He's on his way now. Be safe, Wolf. I'll see you tonight."

As Hawk passes, I surprise him, shifting to meet him chest-to-chest. The speed at which he stiffens is remarkable. I give him a quick pat on the back and end the embrace. Awkward, but a start. "Have a good day. And you stay safe as well."

Back inside the cabin I find my phone plugged in on the kitchen counter. I have a text message from Keyla sitting in the queue. I respond to her question and move to start the coffee.

As I fill the reservoir, I'm pleased I stepped up with Hawk and took a chance. He needs to know he's not on the outside looking in. I lived in that position my entire life.

It's devastating.

~

Hawk

I'm fucking late. As undignified as it is for the man in charge to run, I'm tempted. I should've gotten up and dressed the moment the watch alarm went off and I woke up. I didn't. Calli was burrowed into my side and drooling on my arm with the morning sun catching her hair. The copper and red tones streaked through the gold like hidden fingers of flame. I laid there for far too long, absorbing the warmth of her company and listening as her breath caught in the most mesmerizing feminine sounds. I could've lain there all day.

I wanted to, but...

"You're late," Jayne says, her black Louboutin tapping on the marble tiles. She glares at me from outside the pixie brunch meeting room and checks something off on her tablet.

"It was a late night."

She sneers. "I smell that. Christ, she's all over your skin. Would it have hurt to take a shower?"

It would've hurt me, yes. I like her scent on my skin more than I thought I would. It's not as strong as the mating scent Jaxx and Kotah carry on theirs, but until it fades in a few hours she'll be with me.

"Like I said, late night. Would you like to continue making a scene in the corridor or prove you can do your job and announce my arrival?"

"You're an arrogant prick."

"You're a vindictive bitch. Shall we?"

Jaxx

It's the orgasmic scent of freshly baked cinnamon rolls that raises me from the dead. My mouth is watering, and I swallow a groan. At first, I think it must be a residual of a dream, but nope, my eyes are open, and I still smell it. I stretch and glance around, disoriented. Right. Bastion. I took the couch.

Rolling up to sit, I scrub my fingers over my face and shake myself awake. Unlike Calli, with her phoenix healing ability, I didn't throw off the effects of our drink-fest last night and bounce back. I get the pleasure of the hangover.

"Hey, baby. Get it while it's hot."

Mama? I blink up at the smiling vision of my mother, holding a tray heaped with all the fixin's to fill my empty stomach. With her golden blonde hair swept up, and decked out in a cornflower blue sundress and heels, she is the image of the southern belle she was born.

I set the tray on the coffee table and pat the couch beside me. "I thought you were heading home this morning. Doesn't Daddy have to be at work this afternoon to discuss what he learned at the conference?"

"He does and he did," she says settling in. "He landed a half-hour ago and will go straight to the office from the airport. I stayed to spend time with all y'all. I wanted to stay and get to know everyone. If you don't mind the company, that is."

"Of course not. You're always welcome." My response is twenty-seven years of southern rearing rather than an actual interest in having my mom stay with us during the second week of our mating.

Morning fog plus hangover equals synaptic lag. I love my mom, but I also love spontaneous sex with Calli and the others without worrying about interruptions...

Mama busts up and slaps my leg. "You're priceless, Jaxx. You should see your face. I'm pullin' your leg. I remember how it feels to be newly mated. Good gracious, the last thing I wanted was my parents underfoot. Kotah said you're here until after dinner. When you head out, I'll head home."

I try not to look too relieved. "What time is it now?"

"After one. Still lots of day left to pull up your boots and regroup. Yesterday bucked you good, I hear."

I dig into Mama's home cooking and my cat lets off a contented purr. "It did. I take it Kotah told you?"

"He texted me last night after the fight with his mama. Poor boy. How they don't see Kotah for the gift he is... well, it baffles me."

I nod. "You and he seem to be hitting it off."

"I love him to bits. He hungers for parental love and I'm going to fill him up with it."

That's Mama. She falls in love fast and makes sure every heart has what it needs. "He's an omega. Did you know that?"

Her eyes, the same turquoise as mine, soften with a smile. "It's hard not to sense it the moment you're in the room with him. He has a very soothing soul."

"He does."

I focus on my food, my mind revisiting the loveplay Kotah and I shared. He's so incredibly special. I should never have let

Brant use Kotah's influence to further his investigation. We're trying to build trust within this quint, not betray it.

"You look tired, baby. What's all this weight doing heaped on your shoulders? Are you all right?"

I shrug. "I'm not too proud of myself at the moment."

"Is this about the naked nachos and exposing Jaxx junior to the Fae Prima?"

I choke on my eggs, my cheeks flaring hot. Once I wipe the tears from my eyes, I shake my head, sure I'm as red as the sun-dried tomatoes on my eggs. "Apparently, I need to talk to Kotah about what we *do* and *don't* share with parents."

I pound my chest a couple of times and wash the last of my choking fit down with a swallow of coffee. "No. It's not that. Honestly, after witnessin' how the Prima treats her son, I don't care what she thinks of me."

"All right then, what is it?"

I finish up my last bites and wipe my mouth. "I got caught in the middle between Brant and Hawk. I tried to do right by both and ended up disappointin' them, plus Calli, and likely Kotah too."

She clucks her tongue. "It's as simple as it is hard. If you do someone wrong, you make it right."

"I get that, but the way Calli looked at me last night when it all came to light… it broke my heart."

Mama pats my leg and her expression softens. "I spent the last hour in the kitchen with your phoenix. That girl is as sharp as a tack and filled with sass. I've got all the faith that she sees deep enough into your heart to know you'd never intentionally hurt one of your mates. It'll be fine. You'll see."

I hope so. I don't know what I'll do if this life we're building unravels. "How do you and Daddy do it?"

"Do what, baby?"

"Make mated bliss look easy."

Mama's laughter is a balm to my heartache. She leans sideways and brushes her shoulder with mine. "The key is that we make it *'look'* easy."

She can make light of it all she wants, but my sister and I couldn't have had better role models for building a family. I always knew Laney and I were lucky, but it became more obvious while getting to know my mates. Not one of them had what we had. It makes me sad.

Mama leans in, kisses my cheek, and then wipes it clean. "My best advice on mated bliss is this. Come together with mutual respect, put their needs before your own, and remember to take the time to love and laugh. And when you make a mess of things—and in the beginning, Daddy and I did that quite spectacularly—admit it and ask for forgiveness."

"I can do that."

"Of course, you can," she says, squeezing my hand. "Your mating bond is surely more complicated than most, but you five were chosen for a reason. Put in the time and effort now and you'll reap the reward of happiness for a lifetime."

I hug her tight and breathe in her favorite lilac shampoo. Magdalene Stanton is one in a million. When I pull back, I know what I have to do, and I'm eager to get right to it. "Now, was I dreaming, or do I smell your cinnamon rolls baking?"

"My never-fail cure-all. Guaranteed to fix what ails you."

I grab the breakfast tray and rise to join the others. "Yes ma'am, and just when we need them."

CHAPTER THIRTEEN

Calli

"*H*e did *not*," I say, my mouth hanging open.

"He did, indeed," Maggie says, grinning from ear to ear. "It would've cost a fortune to pull that Charger from the neighbor's pond as well as restore it for water damage *and* pay for the costs to mend the downed fence. John thought it was a better lesson learned to leave Jaxx's first love rotting in silt. It's still down there today as far as I know."

Jaxx sighs. "I loved that car."

"And what about the farmer's daughter?" I ask. "Did you get the girl?"

He winks. "Yeah, baby."

"*Buuut?*" his mom says.

He laughs and licks the icing of his fourth cinnamon roll off his fingers. "Our romance fizzled out soon after. Tearin' up and down the country roads in my car was the biggest draw. Since Daddy grounded me from drivin', she dumped me and took up with Robbie Parkes. He had a blue Impreza."

I lean across the corner of the table and kiss him. "Her loss is my gain."

"Yes ma'am."

I gaze into those turquoise eyes of his and I'm lost. "How could any girl pass you up?"

"That's a mystery for the ages, kitten."

Maggie gathers the dessert plates, rounds the island, and opens the faucet. I rise to help her with the dishes, and she shakes her head. "I've got this. Let me give these a quick rinse and then I'll head out."

"Where are you off to, Mama?"

"I think I'll go for a walk and meet you over at the main lodge for dinner."

"That's not for another three hours," Jaxx says. "That's a long walk."

Maggie finishes in the sink and dries her hands on the tea towel. "I'll manage. There's plenty to keep me busy."

"I'll come with you." The legs of his chair scrape on the floor as he stands. "We can—"

She laughs. "Take the hint, baby. I'm givin' you kids a few hours alone before you're off travelin' again. Love is in the air and I'm the fifth wheel."

Jaxx studies his chair as he tucks it under the table and his cheeks flush an adorable pink. "Okay, that's not embarrassin' or awkward at all. Not even a little."

I laugh. "No? Should I get out your apron from last night? I saved it, you know?"

"*Okaaay*," Jaxx says, closing the distance between us and his laughing mother. He wraps a loving arm around her back and ushers her to the door. "Love you, Mama. Bye-bye, now."

Maggie's laughter is still ringing in the air as one of our security sentinels joins her and they head along the forest path.

When Jaxx gets back from walking his mom out, the cabin

falls quiet. I see the question in his gaze and smile. "Okay, you were right. She's amazing."

"Right?" Jaxx says, his brilliant smile lighting up his face. "I'm glad you guys love her."

"How could we not," Kotah says. "You are truly blessed."

Jaxx shakes his head. "No, Wolf. *We* are. We all are."

～

Brant

The steam from my shower fogs the mirror in a blanket of condensation. I don't wipe it. I have no interest in seeing myself... or anyone else for that matter. Even though Calli's tears healed my physical form, my heart feels like it's been mashed with a meat tenderizer. Why is she so blinded by Hawk?

"Bear," Calli says on the other side of the bathroom door. "Will you come out and join us, please?"

I draw a deep breath, but air doesn't penetrate the pressure blocking my lungs. "Yeah. Be right there."

I tuck the corner of my towel against my hip and head out. The layout of this cabin is far more modest than the four-bedroom, dignitaries one we had last week. Then again, Hawk didn't know he'd have company when he requested it.

The air outside the bathroom is a rude slap of cold against my heated skin. Goosebumps rise and I take it as a sign of what's to come. It's cold shoulder time.

There's no one in the kitchen. I heard Jaxx's mom leave five minutes ago. Maybe Jaxx and Kotah left to escort her to the main lodge.

Face the music time.

Thinking she's on the porch, I slip into the bedroom and grab some pants. Then, I head out and—"Oh, you're in here."

"Yep," Calli says, sitting on the couch with Jaxx lying on the floor, rubbing her feet, and Kotah taking up the armchair.

I round the coffee table and take the empty spot on the couch next to her. The cushion sags under my weight and Calli tilts my way.

She's quiet for a bit and then sighs. "Okay, consider this the only time I give you free rein to badmouth Hawk. Your conviction to your concerns is strong enough that you went behind my back, so tell me what you know for sure, what you suspect, and what you've done."

I scrub my knuckles over the growth on my jaw and lay it all out for her, from the missing kids, to tracing the corruption to the FCO head office, to my girl in accounting tracking large expenditures to Hawk's accounts. "Yes, he explained about his name change, but I'm still left worrying that choking you wasn't an accident."

I wait for her ire to flare and her temper to heat up. It doesn't happen. She doesn't look angry. Worse, she looks sad. "You were there, Brant. You saw his face when he realized he hurt me. That wasn't an act. He was wrecked."

"Or it was a convenient way to get rid of you and when it didn't work, he was genuinely upset. You two were alone in the apartment. Maybe it was a chance he couldn't pass up."

"He wasn't acting," Kotah says. "I touched him with my gift to calm him after Calli collapsed fighting over Jayne. He was devastated. He is emotionally guarded but his heart truly is in the right place. He's committed to us. His love language is just difficult to sort out."

"Not really," Calli says. "He shows us every day. In the arrangements he makes, in the detailed thought he puts into our safety, in the care he takes to make sure we all have what we need."

Spare me. I swallow and fight not to roll my eyes. "I hear what you're saying but you three have no objectivity when it comes to the guardian bond. You think it's a magical, rubber stamp to happily-ever-after. What if it's more than that?"

"More like what?" Jaxx asks.

"No one can argue something seriously twisted is going on. We were chosen to unravel it. There is real evidence pointing at Hawk. Wanting that to be my imagination doesn't change the facts."

Calli nods. "Agreed. There are valid reasons for your concern, and you did what you thought was right, despite knowing it wouldn't be a popular opinion. I respect both your determination and your commitment to those kids."

I hear the giant 'but' hanging in the air. Is that where her understanding ends? "What does that mean going forward?"

"It means, when we get settled tonight in Kotah's village, we'll lay everything out for Hawk and get answers. There will be no more exposing secrets about each other. I'm done with that. Hawk did it and it hurt me. You two did it and it hurt him. Kotah's dragon queen mother did it and hurt him. That's enough. Starting now, we—"

Lukas bolts through the front door and the look on his face has us all jolting to our feet. "Incoming. Get *down!*"

Hawk

"Yes, Minister," I say, yet again. "We all understand your frustrations. What I'm asking is what you'd have us do about them? Instead of pointing at the flaws in the system, perhaps suggest some constructive solutions we can build upon to move forward in the next months."

"Don't pretend you care, Barron," the troll liaison shouts. Spittle sprays the elven aid sitting next to him. "You sit up in your glass tower looking down on the world while—"

"Shut up, Pranton," the goblin king says. "Hawk's right. Stop pointing at the holes in the dike. If it bothers you so much, shove your fat fingers in a few and plug the leak. If anyone's sitting on his perch watching the world from above, it's you."

"Gentlemen, please." I rub my forehead, my head throbbing in earnest. "We've been shouting in circles for an hour. Why don't we take ten minutes and come back to the table with our thinking caps on? Jayne, get the blinds."

I turn off the AV presentation and step out of the way as the pixie queen flies toward the refreshment table. When she passes me, she hovers for a moment. "Ignore them, Sir Barron. My people think you've done an incredible job with the new initiatives."

"Thank you, Queen. That's welcome praise indeed."

The hum of the blinds opening brings the warmth of sunlight into the meeting room. One more hour of this bullshit and I'll rejoin Calli and the others. I reach into my pocket to check if I have any messages at the same time my phone vibrates.

"What is *that?*" the elven aid asks across the room.

"By the Powers, is it a *fire?*"

I follow the pixie queen's pointed finger and my muscles freeze. A sickening panic erupts hot in my veins as black smoke plumes up from behind the treetops.

"That's at the compound," someone shouts.

"Are we under attack?"

I race out of the meeting room to the balcony at the end of the corridor. I push through the glass door and keep running. The late-afternoon air hits my face like a wall of stale, hot air as I dive from the eighth-floor platform and transform in freefall. I pump my wings, my hawk shrieking a shrill cry of fury.

Yes, we're under attack.

Fuck. Fuck. Fuck. The cabin is ablaze. It's blown to a scattered heap of kindling and the burning wood is sending a choking black smoke billowing skyward. Where are they? My heart hammers as I circle above. My security team is there, scrambling around the edges of the blaze, searching for a way in. They don't see the opening I do—well done, Lukas.

From my vantage point, I see the only way in. With a great push, I propel myself toward the ground and sweep back my wings to cut through the smoke as quickly as I can.

I suck in a last breath of air before hitting the wall of heat. The supply of oxygen doesn't last long. Within moments, my lungs burn, my eyes water, and my skin is bubbling in blisters.

Motherfucking hell.

Finding Lukas's shield blind is a matter of tracking his energy. He's been with me long enough for me to recognize his magical signature, even in the blinding pitch.

When I bump up against it, I spin and press my back to the dome he erected. He would've focused on Calli. I can only hope the others are in there too.

Throwing my arms out, I send out a pulse to clear a path. Nothing. The carnage is unruly. It refuses to relinquish its hold.

I choke and char singes my lungs. I turn my face to breathe through the fabric covering my shoulder. It does little to filter the smoke. Can Calli breathe? I should've been here instead of refereeing a losing battle between pompous windbags.

Senseless. Stupid. So-fucking-unimportant.

Still, I can't help them if I choke to death.

Magic surges and snaps in my fingertips. I create a vortex around me, forcing smoke away while funneling oxygen down from the heavens. I gulp in a breath and cough against the damage done. Again, I think of Calli suffering.

And me not being here for her.

With a cry of rage, I focus on the debris preventing my mate from escaping this hell. My pulse didn't work. I need to try something different.

If I can't move the fire, I'll move the fucking building.

I send another wave of energy outward. The weight of the building's debris tests every magical muscle I possess, but soon, I feel a shift. It's moving.

It's working... just not fast enough.

Turning things up full-blast, I push my limits and access the total release of my bottled-up powers. I've always governed myself to about sixty percent of my potential. Magical ability in wildlings is unusual and dangerous. I've always kept my powers tightly reined, but if I want them out of this fire, I have to give more.

Harnessing my full potential, I push to my limits and force my will to burst from me like the most powerful orgasm ever.

Power burns in my cells and explodes.

My world detonates. Somewhere in my distant mind, I know I need to pull back or burn myself up completely. I can't.

If it means Calli's life... I'll pay any price.

CHAPTER FOURTEEN

Calli

A sleeping Hawk is a beautiful Hawk. Considering this is the third time I've had the pleasure of sharing time with him when he's not fully guarded, I consider myself on one hell of a winning curve. The first time was the nap that ended with his hands clenched around my throat. The second was when I climbed into bed with him in the cabin. It held a startlingly domestic warmth to it but when I woke, he was gone. The third, this time, I'm not letting him get away.

Naked, with a chenille blanket draped at his waist, he remains unconscious in the aft stateroom of his plane. Hawk is sex incarnate. I finally get the chance to study the inked sleeves that run from his elbows up to and over his shoulders. Beautifully designed in black and gray, only a very select few key images are highlighted with a flourish of color.

I'm no expert on fae history, but the intertwining depictions look like a violent tale of fae mythology.

And then there's the platinum nipple ring. I've never been one for tattoos and piercings but on Hawk it works. It's almost worth him being rendered unconscious so I can perform my Florence Nightingale routine.

Warm water in a basin. A velvety soft washcloth. A need to ease some of his discomforts even if it's the most superficial of all his suffering. It's hard work cleaning all the hard, flat planes and rolling, muscular bulges of Hawk's sooty bod.

I've never loved a task quite as much.

I douse the little cloth and wring out the excess for another pass on his neck and chest. His biceps are damn impressive. The same goes for the corded muscle that tapers in the man-V from his hips down to his groin. Holy-schmoly, is it wrong to be breathless and randy while he's still out cold?

I gasp when his hand closes on my wrist.

His eyes pop wide and his breathing stops.

"It's okay, broody. It's just me."

His gaze shifts to me but he looks no less alarmed. "Why am I waking up here?"

"You overdid it with the magical rescue and collapsed in the rubble."

"Did you heal me?"

I shake my head. "No. A little blue lady with silver wings did that."

He releases my hand and his focus sharpens. "The pixie queen? Shit Calli, you can't accept favors from certain species—"

I place my palm on his chest to keep him from lurching up too soon. "Relax. Lukas handled everything. He said you wouldn't honor any debt to her. She healed you without expectation of repayment."

He swallows and relaxes back onto the bed. Well, if Hawk ever truly relaxes. "What are you doing?"

I warm my cloth in the basin and continue my work. "You were smoky from the explosion. Since you were in no condition to have a shower, I took liberties.

His grip shifts down to the sheet covering his hips. "Did everyone make it out safely?"

"Yes. Thank you for that." I bend and press a kiss on the soft flesh of his temple. "Jaxx's mom and Doc got swept up in our evacuation, so they're here with us too. And Brant's a little disgruntled that you pulled our asses from the fire using magic, but it is what it is."

"And you were all safely contained?"

I nod. "The four of us were talking in the living room when Lukas rushed in. He saw the missile coming in and domed us in a magical shield. It was an inferno and suffocating in there, but we walked away from it, so nothing to complain about."

"Where's Lukas now?"

"He evacuated us and stayed behind to investigate the attack. He said he'll follow when he has something to report."

Hawk remains quiet as he processes and then tilts his head to the basin. "And the bedside care?"

I nip at my bottom lip. He's told me a bunch of times that this isn't what he wants. Maybe taking liberties wasn't such a good idea. "I was curious to touch you. Are you angry?"

"No," he murmurs, a wicked grin curving his lips. "Have your curiosities been met?"

"Not really. No."

"Then perhaps you should continue your work."

I hide my giddy grin by dropping my gaze and repeating the douse and wring routine.

"You look pleased with yourself, Spitfire."

I shrug one shoulder and focus on cleaning around the ring of platinum. "Someone recently told me I have a problem with personal boundaries."

He laughs and his six-pack flexes under my fingers. "I think you proved my point."

I sweep the cloth down the rock-hard ridges of his stomach

and ease the sheet a little further south. "Does it bother you? Me pushing in on you?"

There's a beat of silence, and then he relaxes a bit more. "I think I've lost my edge on holding you at arm's reach. I admit you're not at all what I imagined. I, too, am curious about a few things."

"Like?"

His grin grows more heated and he shakes his head. "I don't like being told the answers. I'll figure them out myself."

I swallow, my heart racing as my gaze slides over him. I am riveted by this side of the man. The teasing. His firmly etched scowl replaced by a smile. He is savagely handsome. "Might these curiosities involve us being naked?"

His possessive gaze washes over me like a rush of warm water. "A good many of them, yes."

"Then, since we've got nowhere else to be for the next hour, maybe we should try to find some of those answers."

"I think I'd like to finish my bath first. If you don't mind?"

First. That means that after that...

I warm the cloth in the basin and dive in for the big finish. I start at his shoulders and descend the slope of his pecs and abs. Gawd, he's beautiful.

I dip my hand under the sheet to brush his navel.

He hisses, and I press my luck.

Drawing the sheet down toward his knees, I uncover the grand prize. He's fully aroused. Massively erect. "You don't mind, do you? I don't want to get the sheet wet." I swallow and continue the sponge bath.

"No, please. Whatever you do, spare the sheets. One question, though. How did I get soot down there? I was wearing clothes if I remember."

I bite my lip and wipe down his beautiful cock and swipe the cloth over his sac and between his legs. "What can I say... I'm a dedicated caregiver. I pride myself on being thorough."

~

Hawk

Thorough? Ha. My mate is a minx, toying with me... Calli runs that velvety heat up the inside of my legs to the juncture of my groin, and my heart stutters in my chest. This is new territory for me. I never allow females the freedom to explore my body. As a Dom, I have an unwavering need to be the one in control. Being in power is the way I get off.

Not with her.

Yes, she's taking her liberties, but her fascination with my body has my animal side rearing up and begging for more. For the first time, that pungent feminine scent of arousal is intended for me. Only me.

"Tell me, Calli," I say, my voice a deep rasp. "Are you a member of the mile-high club?"

That sweeping cloth stops dead and her cheeks flush. "No. I'd never been on a plane before I met you."

I expect her to shoot the question back at me, but she doesn't. It doesn't take my skills in reading people to figure out why. "Despite what you're thinking, neither am I."

Her brow pinches like she doesn't believe me.

It goes to show how little we know about one another. And while I hate explaining myself, to build trust with Calli, I make an exception. "When I travel by plane, I'm on business and focused on reviewing a presentation or solving a problem. My plane is for work."

Her lips purse together. "Jayne was work and play."

I wrinkle my nose. "Jayne was work, a sexual outlet, and access to a powerful network of old-world fae power. She has never been play."

Calli looks skeptical. I take the cloth from her hand and remove the basin from the bed. Reaching above the bedding

platform, I set them on the console. "Calli, until now, my part-
ners either served as personal sexual gratification or a
strategic maneuver. Nothing wagered. Nothing invested. None
of them have ever been lovers in the sense of what you
imagine."

"Which is why you don't want to get tangled up with me,
right? The mating bond threatens to blur that line."

I scoff. "It's too late for that. As much as my hunger for you
might be influenced by the mating bond, me enjoying you as a
person and wanting more of that connection is all you. You are
an enigma. I find you frustratingly irresistible."

The smile she rewards me with is worth more than ten times
my amassed fortune. "That's a boldly affectionate statement
from a guy who insists there's no inner romantic version of
himself to coax out."

True. I don't know where this version of me comes from.

Maybe Calli isn't the only one transforming. "So, back to the
mile-high club," I say, refusing the distraction. "Shall we
christen this stateroom or wait until we've got more time to
explore our curiosities?"

Calli tilts her head this way and that. "Well, you're stuck here
without your leather and chains. If we seize the moment, you'll
have to keep it simple. I wouldn't want you to be bored."

I run my hands around her waist and pull her down to lay
beside me. She comes willingly and I roll over her, so she's
under my power. "You never bore me, Spitfire. I think we could
occupy ourselves enough to keep things interesting."

Her emerald gaze swirls with the flames of her wild side and
my hawk rises to the fore. "I'm not letting you off the hook. I
want the full Hawk Barron treatment soon. Then, it'll be my
turn to tie *you* up. I'm going to make you beg, Barron."

Her fiery determination warms my cold, misbehaving heart.
Calliope Tannis, where did you come from? "I look forward to
you trying."

Jaxx

I knock on the pocket door of the stateroom and clear my throat. "I'm sorry, you two. I hate to cockblock you, but I need Hawk. I wouldn't interrupt except it's an emergency."

"Come." The response comes quickly but not without a growl lacing his tone.

The pocket door whispers on its track and I feel slightly better when I take in the scene. Calli is clothed and although Hawk is fully aroused, he only looks moderately annoyed.

"Yeah, sorry, you two. I think I royally fucked up and need your help."

Hawk sits up and props his palms on the bed behind him. "How so? What's happened?"

With Hawk running the Monster Rights Conference, there hasn't been time to fill him in on Brant's quest to find the three missing kids until now, so I start there. I explain our working theory that someone powerful and high up in the FCO erased them from society. Then, I explain how Brant followed the financial trail of one of the FCO cleaners back to Hawk's office.

"And someone from *my* office had those parents' minds wiped of all memory?"

"Parents, teachers, neighbors… it's broad and extensive."

"Toss me some pants," he says, pointing to the duffle Lukas left for him before we took off. The guy looks pissed, and honestly, I'm glad. That kind of fury isn't easily feigned, and it makes me surer than ever that Hawk isn't the Black Knight. "Who was the cleaner, Fiske, or Torbie?"

"Alexander Fiske." I pull a pair of black khakis from the bag and toss them over. Calli looks disappointed that he's getting dressed, but I can't help it. I need the guy.

"Fiske has a powerful gift and can affect large areas at once.

Unlike most fae with neuro-manipulation abilities, he doesn't need direct contact with each person he wipes. He can send out a message on a cognitive frequency that encompasses a radius of a small town. That does the work for him."

"Explains how thorough it was."

He pulls on his pants and I catch an eyeful of the guy's inkwork. Man, Hawk's arms and back are a living tribute to our heritage. It's breathtaking. Hawk catches me gawking and it doesn't seem open for comment.

Hawk shifts to his knees to make his way over. With the two plush couches pulled down into a bed, there's no floor space to maneuver. "Fiske is a solid company man. I doubt very much he's involved in a powerplay conspiracy. I'd bet my left nut whoever is behind this convinced him it was a sanctioned job."

"So, you can talk to him?"

I hand him the stretch t-shirt and he pulls it over his chest. "Now that you're involving me in your concerns, I can do a lot of things. Still, I don't see your emergency?"

I rap my knuckles against the tightness in my chest. "I think when I asked my dad to search the names from the database in his office, someone took notice. He landed at Bergstrom before noon this morning and told my mom he was headed straight into the office. He never arrived and isn't answering his cell. Mama had a neighbor go to the house and he's not there either. Brant and I checked with police and hospitals and nothing. I'm worried, Hawk. I think someone might've taken him."

CHAPTER FIFTEEN

Kotah

*B*y the time the plane lands and we disembark, Hawk, Jaxx, and Brant have a working plan on how to confirm whether or not John Stanton is truly missing. Needless to say, Jaxx's mama is beside herself, though no one without a high level of empathic sensitivity would know that. She is an admirably strong female and wears a convincing veil of unshaken confidence.

Our group is walking across the tarmac when the pilot shouts for Hawk's attention. We turn back and are looking up the stairs when he hauls my sister out of the plane door. "We have a stowaway, sir."

Hawk looks at her and then me.

I shake my head. "I didn't know, but I'll find out."

Keyla pulls her arm out of the grasp of the pilot. He seems genuinely insulted that someone snuck onto the plane unin-vited. She seems equally insulted to be detained and handled like the interloper she is.

With her freedom reclaimed, Keyla descends the stairs and rushes forward, chin high and back straight. When did she become such a royal? Or royal pain in the ass is closer to the truth. "Before anyone reacts, know that Kotah didn't know I hid aboard and tagged along."

"Why did you?" I ask. "Mother will lose her mind."

Keyla waves her hand in the air. "She'll get over it. I'll say I came to ensure you comply with her command. Blah, blah... she'll eat it up."

She likely will.

"And why are you here?" Calli asks.

I see a flash of the little girl I used to shield from the world, the one who depended on me to show her the way and protect her from our parents and the disingenuous world of being born a royal. When Father shipped me to university, I saw it as a miraculous taste of freedom. I suppose, me being gone meant something different for her.

She had to adapt and fend for herself.

"You know what?" I say, offering her my hand. "All that matters is that you're here now. I'll call Mother when we arrive at the village and we'll smooth it over together." I wrap my arm around her shoulders, turn her toward the awaiting truck, and kiss the side of her head. "It'll be fine."

Calli and Hawk don't look so sure.

If Keyla is reaching out, there is no chance I'll leave her to fend for herself again. Like I said, It'll be fine. They'll see.

"Welcome to the Northwood corridor," I say as we get out of the truck in the graveled parking lot at the edge of the village. Beyond the line of vehicles parked in the secluded lot, a solid wall of greenery rises from the rich earth. "Twenty-two-hundred acres of protected and private land. My ancestors declared this entire wildlife corridor was to remain preserved. No cars. No pollution. Only the beauty of nature and space to enjoy it."

Calli hugs my arm and rests her cheek on my shoulder. "It's wonderful. No wonder you never felt at home in that fancy fae palace. This place is much more you."

True. Potential energy buzzes in my blood as I breathe in the clean, fresh air of my home. It calls to my wolf and brings me a sense of belonging and peace I only ever feel when I'm here. "Into the woods I go, to lose my mind and find my soul."

"My sweet poet," Calli says, smiling up at me.

I cast a glance at the others to see if they feel the infusion of energy too. Despite the raw feelings of disappointment and mistrust between the guys over the past two days, they seem genuinely appeased for the moment.

Brant lifts his face and sniffs the air. "I can see how this place could get under your skin. It's magical."

"Naturally and elementally," Hawk says.

"What do you mean?" Calli asks.

He rounds the front of the truck and presses his palm flat against the ground. "The power of ley lines running beneath the ground is palpable. This land is rich with fae energy."

"Maybe that's why your ancestors first settled here," Jaxx says, studying the sinking sun and the swirling coral skyline. "And why they preserved it from cars and modernizations."

"Or maybe they were stuffy and stubborn and got their kicks by making life more difficult," Keyla says. When we all turn to look at her, she shrugs. "Just offering an opposing opinion after growing up here."

Footsteps approach from the main path and Hawk and Brant circle back to stand in front of Calli.

"Be at ease," I say, recognizing the scent on the breeze.

Logan Silver Fox steps out of the growing shadows of the trees. He's a mid-sixties male with faded blue eyes and skin as black as the night quickly falling upon us. He's the male in charge of the village in the absence of a Northwood family member on-premises, and the male who oversaw Keyla and me throughout the years of our upbringing.

He studies our group, places his arm across his middle, and bows low. "Prince Nakotah, Princess Nakeyla, welcome home, children. Everything is in order, young majesties. Please, everyone, follow me."

Calli

Northwood Village is as quaint and rustic as it is awe-inspiring. Similar to the setup of the Bastion, Kotah's home compound is comprised of chinked wooden cabins peppered throughout the wilds of treed lands, with well-trodden paths leading to and from a main courtyard and lodge.

Logan Silver Fox speaks quietly with Kotah about the accommodations and preparations and leads us to Northwood Hall, the home of the founding family. Nightfall is taking hold by the time we arrive and the flickering flame of torches lights our way. It's surreal.

I'm not sure what I expect of Northwood Hall, knowing it is the familial home of the Prima and Prime, but I'm pleasantly surprised. Unlike Kotah's cold and distant parents, his ancestral home bursts with the warmth of honeyed-pine construction, slate floors, ruby and gold accents, and the welcoming energy that Kotah exudes.

"You like it?" Kotah asks twenty minutes later.

He comes up behind me where I'm leaning over the second-floor railing taking in the great room and glass window wall below. There is no electricity. The interior is lit by dozens of ivory candles making things seem even more magical.

He wraps me in a playful embrace from behind, cupping my

breasts and kissing the back of my neck. His cock is solid against my ass and he grinds gently growling in my ear. "I want you naked, Calli. I need inside you. I want to claim you, here, where I feel the most myself."

I turn in his arms and the sexual excitement between us raises the hair on my arms. I swallow and my body responds to his need. My nipples tighten, the brush of my t-shirt over their sensitive peaks a delectable friction. "What about your sister and Jaxx's mom?"

My shirt rucks up and warm hands push the fabric out of his way. "I asked Brant and Doc to take Keyla for a night run and Jaxx to start a bonfire in the pit out back. They've given us the house. I can't help myself, *Chigua*. My wolf needs inside you, to mark my mate, here in my home."

He dips me backward, kissing my sternum and reaching into the front of my pants. I groan as greedy fingers find the damp heat of my core. I'm lost to his passion.

"Whatever you need, sweet wolf. Strip me down and soothe your pangs of hunger."

Hawk

As the scent of the bonfire builds in the yard and Calli's sexy feminine sounds and scents build above, I marvel that being intertwined within this group dynamic isn't making me more agitated. I've always cherished my singularity but now that I'm resolved to seeing where this mating takes us, the nearness of the other four doesn't trigger my aggression—not even when the wolf is taking my place devouring Calli's body.

We almost got there.

I don't blame Jaxx for interrupting us. Now that I consider

Calli mine to claim, the predator in me is enjoying the thrill of the chase. I'm savoring the burn of anticipation. If Calli wants the full Hawk Barron experience, I want the time to plan something unique.

With all kinds of erotic images bombarding my brain, I buckle down my need for her and get to work. Busy. Busy. Assassins to catch, traitors to uncover, a father to find, two worlds to safeguard. No pressure.

I tap on the keyboard of my laptop and get things fired up. If Alexander Fiske was contracted by the FCO to wipe three towns on the west coast there will be mission orders in his file. Scanning through his company logs, I'm more alarmed by what I find than I expect.

My signature?

It's as plain as the ink on the scanned page. For anyone who cares to look, I ordered the djinn to wipe families of their children… and not just the three Brant is aware of… Fiske has performed his task on fourteen different occasions over the past ten months.

Motherfucker… okay, now I'm seriously pissed.

Brant

Doc, Keyla, and I get back from our romp in the forest and shift back to our human forms to join Jaxx and his mom at the fire pit. The two of them are understandably distraught over Jaxx's missing father, but until Lukas or his Texas team checks back, there's nothing much to do. Hawk has someone in the police department checking traffic cams to figure out where John Stanton went missing and maybe we'll get lucky and get a clue as to who took him.

If anyone did take him.

Calli and Kotah open the double glass doors off the great room and step onto the back patio. Calli has a tray of plates, salad, and cutlery and the kid is weighed down with platters of meat stacked a mile high.

I head over to see if I can help with the grub and—my bear lets off a rumble. "Damn, you two smell sexy. Did you enjoy your private time?"

"Very much," Calli says, still caught in the post-coitus afterglow. "I think we christened the place thoroughly."

Kotah chuckles and lights the barbeque. The thing is a stainless-steel masterpiece of grilling, searing, boiler options, and the airy *poof* it lets off as it ignites makes me salivate. "The two of us set a standard, yes. I'm hoping for a repeat performance with the rest of us, though. Call me greedy, but Calli, Jaxx, and I have mated, if we want to be a true quint, you and Hawk need to join the fun at some point too."

Hmmph. I have serious doubts Hawk and I will get to a point where either of us will ever want to go there. "Let's see how things play out, 'kay, Wolf?"

Calli opens her mouth to comment when Hawk strides outside with his phone extended. "Maggie. I have someone who'd like to speak with you."

Jaxx's mom rises from her seat at the fire and rushes to take the phone. "John? John, is that you?"

When she cradles the phone against her ear and tears start to fall, Jaxx wraps an arm around her and they step away.

"You did it," Calli says.

Hawk shrugs. "Not really. We tracked his travel from the airport to the office and lost him in the building's parking garage. Then, a half-hour ago, he stepped into the office confused and without any recollection of the past six hours."

"Interrogated and wiped," I say.

Hawk nods. "Thankfully, he didn't know the details of your suspicions. He couldn't tell them much and they would've raised more suspicion by making him disappear than simply wiping his memory and setting him loose."

"He's safe," Calli says. "That's the important part."

Hawk meets her gaze. "Until we figure out who's behind this, no one is safe, Spitfire. I called in a favor and John and Jaxx's older sister, Laney, are being escorted to the airport now to board a private jet owned by a colleague of mine. They'll be here tonight." He shifts his gaze to Kotah. "Any chance we can arrange a family cabin for the Stantons close by?"

"I'll take care of it," Keyla says, joining the conversation. "Those are our guesthouses." She points into the darkness toward the twin roof peaks silhouetting the moon behind a low rise. "I'll get one prepped for Jaxx's family."

"I'll help," Calli says, setting the plates on the grill center countertop. "As long as you promise to call us before Brant eats everything."

"No promises," I say, winking at her.

Her smile isn't as easy as it was a few days ago and that hurts. We talked out our difference of opinion on Hawk back at the Bastion cabin, but all is not yet forgotten.

Kotah and I watch the girls following the torch-lit path and I chuckle. "I thought Calli wanted to strangle your sister."

The kid smiles, laying out steaks and ribs on the barbeque. "Calli possesses a tremendous capacity for forgiveness—and good thing, too. We've all benefited from it already and it's only been two weeks."

Hawk chuffs. "Hopefully, we can smooth out some bumps in the road going forward so we won't need to keep seeking forgiveness. I'm willing to work on being more of a team player if you guys stop looking at me like I'm the scum polluting your favorite pond."

Kotah passes Hawk a beer from the cooler and smiles. "I don't see you that way and I'd very much like to have you more involved. I was just saying so when you joined us."

I don't trust the guy, but for the sake of the others, I have to give him a chance. "I still think you're an arrogant jackass."

Hawk's smile is cocky and not at all offended. "But not with people inside my circle of trust. The question is, do you want to stay on the outside of that circle or not?"

After thinking about it, I scratch my balls good and offer him the hand to shake.

He rolls his eyes but accepts the gesture.

I'm not sure if Jaxx hears the tail end of that convo or if it's coincidental timing, but the jaguar returns, steps right up to Hawk, and gives the guy a bro hug. "Thank you," he says. After a couple of firm hand-slaps on Hawk's back, he eases off. "Daddy and Laney are on their way here, and Mama and I couldn't be more relieved. I owe you big."

"You're both welco—" Hawk's words cut off as Mama pulls him in for a second Stanton hug, this one accompanied by a lipstick smudging kiss to his cheek.

"Oh, my sweet boy," Mama says, rubbing his face with her thumb. "You did an old girl's heart proud. Thank you."

Hawk's wide-eye, shell-shocked gaze makes my day.

Kotah pauses the tongs over the grill and tilts his head toward the cabin. "My sister and Calli are preparing one of the guest cabins for you and your family, Mama. If you'd like, I'll walk you over as soon as I turn the meat."

"No need, hon. I'll find my way just fine. You boys stay and sort yourselves out." She starts off, and then turns to smile over her shoulder at us. "Remember, there are a lot of emotions in the early days of mating. Give yourselves the space to err and the time to build an understanding of one another. If you all give a little and get a little in return, it'll work out in the end."

When Maggie starts to move out, I meet Doc's gaze and signal for him to escort her. Kotah's village might be secluded and feel safe, but like Hawk says, until we know more, none of us are safe.

The *sizzle* of meat and the *crack* of the fire are the only sounds floating between the four of us while we let that sink in.

Give a little and get a little. I suppose I can try.

I turn to the avian and drop my attitude. "So, Hawk. Were you able to find out anything about those missing kids?"

CHAPTER SIXTEEN

Calli

*T*he next morning, my phone alarm vibrates against the bedside table and I swipe the screen to make it stop. Brant is curled up in his grizzly form at the end of the bed. Nakotah is sexy as hell sprawled naked with me in a tangle of rumpled sheets cascading to the floor. Jaxx is sadly missed. He crashed at the Stanton cabin after he and Hawk picked up John and Laney from the airport in the middle of the night. And Hawk is in the next bedroom, unwilling to risk sleeping with me since his sleep sedatives blew up in the cabin explosion.

Rolling off the mattress, I snag one of the sheets from the floor and wrap it around me. When Kotah stirs, I blow him a kiss. "Going to ambush Hawk in the shower."

Kotah nods. "Good luck, *Chigua*."

I pee and brush my teeth in the master ensuite before shuffling next door. The door is closed but not locked, so I let myself in. The hiss of water in the bathroom draws me past the neatly made bed to the partially closed door. I push it open and absorb the visual.

Hawk has his back to me, his arm braced against the marble wall of the shower. His head is dropped as water rushes down his body and caresses over all the inked landscape, cut ridges, and honed muscles.

Gawd he's such a sexy badass.

Warm tingles spread across my skin and bring me fully awake. Is it the growing heat of the bathroom or the male in front of me that has me flushed and wanting to drop my sheet?

It's him... definitely.

It hurt to think he might cut ties with us. It was a pain I endured with the hope that he would see in time, he belongs with us. Is it wrong to want to solidify his wavering affection? Will he resent me for trying to seduce him?

Again.

"Are you planning to stand there and ogle me all morning, or are you joining me? You wash my back and I'll wash yours."

Done deal. I drop the sheet and rush to join him behind the foggy glass wall. I rush a little too much and slip when I hit the shower floor. Hawk's arms come around me in a split-second, his wet hands making it tough to get a solid hold.

He grips and gropes me quite spectacularly before I stand before him steady and breathless. "Nothing like making an entrance, right?"

Hawk taps an electronic control panel and activates a program for the front and back nozzles. He has that 'I'll take care of everything' look on his face that I'm growing to count on. I don't care what he has in mind, he has free reign to claim my body and soul.

"Although, ogling you all morning wouldn't have been a sacrifice either."

Circling behind me, he presses tight and shifts me under the spray. The water is warm, maybe a touch hot, as it hits my chest and runs down my breasts. His hands slide around my ribs and across my navel. I drop my head back and he nips my neck. "I'm supposed to meet Jaxx and Brant. We have a long day of sleuthing ahead."

"Brant's still asleep. Take a bit of time and indulge."

He pulls me tighter against his hips and his cock presses hard against my lower back. I groan, thankful he's got such a firm grip on me. "I suppose it can't hurt to start the day off on the right foot."

"Right? You know... release some of that tension you always seem to carry."

His palm makes its way to my mons and his fingers delve between my legs. Simultaneously his other arm grips me tight under my breasts. "What happened to the full Hawk Barron experience, Spitfire? A quick fuck in the shower seems awfully vanilla by comparison."

I buck as he tweaks my clit and my right nipple at the same time. "I have a feeling nothing about sex with you is vanilla. Besides, you can always dress up vanilla with a little caramel and whipped cream."

He grinds against my ass and my knees threaten to give out. He holds me firm and chuckles in my ear. "Don't get weak in the knees yet. You challenged me to be myself with you, remember? I'm an alpha and a dom. Raise the bar. Whipped cream is mainstream. Think harder. How do you want to dress up vanilla?"

"Kotah could watch."

"Do you get off on voyeurism?"

He takes that moment to rub over my cleft with more ardor and my breath catches. "Since the mating, yes."

"Being reborn a wildling is bound to unleash your primal side. Okay, what else dresses up vanilla."

"Hot fudge."

"Mmm, how hot? Does it sting when I spoon it onto your nipples?"

I stiffen. "Should it?"

"Oh yeah, I think it should." He reaches in front of me and turns the faucet a touch, so the water gets hotter. "Tell me if you don't like something, Calli. We're playing so you should always enjoy what we share. You're safe with me but for kink to work for both of us, you have to trust me and be honest about your pleasures. Do you understand?"

The water grows hotter and it's almost too much… almost. It heats the air and makes me feel a little light-headed.

"Do you understand?" he repeats in my ear.

"Yes." I swallow and try to focus. His hands are everywhere and I'm throbbing with the need for him to push inside me. "Do I need a safe word?"

"Of course," he says, nipping his way from one shoulder, across my nape to the other shoulder. "We'll develop one as we progress. For now, just tell me to stop if it's too much. I won't push you far until we set some boundaries. As I said, you're safe with me. Do you trust me?"

"Yes."

"Good girl," he says reaching around to the faucet again.

I'm afraid he's going to turn it up again, but he doesn't. He turns it down. The water that hits me next is cool and I suddenly miss the heat. I step back but he stops me. "No, no. Trust me. I'll make you feel good. Do you like heat more than cold?"

I swallow and nod. "Yes."

"Do you want me to give you back heat?"

"Yes."

"All right, then. Step up on the tile footings, angel, and spread your legs."

He points to the floor of the shower and I see what he wants. There's a tile ledge on both sides of the shower where the tile meets the wall on one side and thick glass on the other. It's wide, maybe three feet apart but I do as I'm told.

"Good girl, now lean forward and press your palms on the wall in front of you."

Hawk

Fuck. Fuck. Fuck. Calli will be my undoing, I swear. I planned to give her a few orgasms and leave her wanting more for later. There's no way. Maybe it is mating madness, but as I pull my fingers from her clenching heat, my mind shatters. Calli's hunger pollutes the enclosed space and I need inside her more than I've ever needed anything.

As she leans forward, I stare at the meaty rounds of her ass, and my cock pulses like a divining rod, pointing toward gold. I smell her vulnerability. Her compliance gives me a stunning sense of how obedient she can be when she tries. My original plan dissolves as my control breaks. I suck my two fingers into my mouth and savor her flavor as I hit the control pad.

The front nozzle shuts off and four side nozzles start, two on our left and two on our right. They spray with a jet pulse, the water steamy warm again.

She groans and arches like a cat in heat. "Gawd, that feels so nice."

Good. I need her to love playing sex games. I need her to be able to fulfill this part of me. For the first time in two weeks, I wonder if everything might work out, after all. "Now, close your eyes and don't open them no matter how much you want to. It's just you and me in here, so let your senses wander and feel, got it?"

She nods.

Damn. She's so much more responsive than I expected. I give my cock a couple of tugs and yeah, I'm as hard as I've been all week. "You ready?"

"Yes," she says, her voice breathy.

"You're not going to pass out on me, are you?"

"Gawd, I hope not." There's a touch of laughter in her voice and it eases my concern a little.

"If you feel faint, I'm trusting you to tell me, yes?"

"Yes."

"Good girl. Eyes closed. Here we go."

A mewling sound escapes her throat as I reach under her from behind and reinsert my two fingers. Her pussy is tight and wet and so greedy with its pulse and squeeze. Despite the height difference, with her perched on the baseboard ledge, our bodies match up perfectly.

She shudders as I stroke her, arching, surging, moving against the sensation of my touch. The need burning inside me rises with every brush of her skin. It calls out to the darkest part of me demanding I claim her.

Is this it? Am I ready to accept this mating and all that comes with it? Being bound and responsible for four mates?

Calli's head drops forward, her legs trembling in a gentle quiver. She's close. "Not yet, angel. Hold off a little longer. I'll tell you when."

Her growl shoots straight to my cock.

I chuckle. "Brace yourself."

She takes my command seriously and strengthens her position against the shower wall. Having her stretched out and compliant is erotic as hell. I release the nozzle warming my hip and bring it around to spray her clit.

Angling the pulsing jets to massage her feminine folds, I work my fingers in her core. Hot water spills over my hands and down the inside of her legs. Calli cries out and bursts into a blinding golden glow. "Oh… I need to come."

"Not yet," I say, my breath coming fast. "How good do you feel?"

"So good… too good."

I slip a third finger inside her and stretch her wider. I'm a big boy and want her ready for me. The extra digit does her in and I feel her muscles trigger her orgasm.

Damn. She's so fucking responsive.

"Okay, angel. Let it take you. Feel it wash through you and let yourself explode. I've got you."

I set the nozzle back in its cradle and hold her steady through her release. Her cries echo off the hard surfaces and I memorize every sound she makes. Slowing my fingers, we ride out the waves of her first orgasm.

When she settles, I turn down the water pressure.

"You up for me now?" I step in tight, angle her a little deeper in her stance and guide my aching cock where it so desperately wants to go. "I want to fuck you, Calli. I need to fuck you. Are you good with that?"

"Yes," she gasps, her voice pitchy.

"Tell me you want it."

"Hawk... please... yes, I want you to fuck me." She bounces on her feet as if impatient and I lose another ounce of my control. *My undoing, I swear.*

I press the head of my cock through her opening and bury deep inside her. I freeze. My skin burns, my arms start to shake, and I feel the magic of our mating bond taking hold. The relief that has eluded me the past weeks hits hard and fast. It is the harshest ecstasy and the sweetest pain.

For better or for worse, Calli is my mate now. With my animal side locking into place, I know it's forever. *"Mine."*

I hear my words echo in the shower and they startle me. With Calli I lose control. I withdraw my hips a few inches and press home. "Fuck, you feel good."

Like she said—so good... too good.

I close my eyes and focus on my breath. In. Out. In. Out—

The succulence of the heat ripping through my cells makes

my head spin. And that's before I start to pick up my pace. As fae magic tightens its hold on me, I try not to fight it.

I want this... I think. No, I'm sure... pretty sure.

The only thing I'm truly sure about is that I want Calli.

If being part of the guardian's mating quint is how I make that happen, then it's done. Gripping her hips, I thrust hard, burying myself inside her again and again.

Fuck, she even feels like home.

I don't know how long I last. It could be minutes. It could be hours. I'm lost in the consuming bliss of mating my female. Calli meets every hammering thrust with a buck of her hips, every grunt of mine with a gasp of her own, every slide, and glide with a clench and release.

I'm oblivious to the world around me, the dangers we face, and the demands on my time and attention.

For this moment... there is only this moment.

Eventually, though, my balls crawl so damn tight into my crotch that I'm sure they'll implode. And as much fun as we are having, I don't want to hurt her or have her blacking out. The animal in me gained strength today.

I feel the power of our union feeding my cells already.

I clench my jaw as my release ignites in my balls, building pressure in my shaft. I push back, fighting a losing battle.

Calli's pussy is greedy and the throbbing of her next orgasm starts. Another shock wave shoots to my cock and a ragged cry rips from my throat. It echoes off the marble and glass. There is no holding back.

My orgasm breaks free. Heated jets pour into my mate as my hawk shrieks victory inside my soul.

Calli shouts my name and comes apart with me.

Glowing with the power of her gift, she's breathtaking. She breaks through every barrier I erected, and we crash together into an abyss. Pleasure doesn't begin to describe it. I am home. I never want to pull out. I never want to leave her warmth.

I stay inside her and release her hips, afraid my grip will bruise her. I collapse against her back, my arms wrapping around her to hold her up. I kiss the sweat and shower slick skin of her shoulder blades. Another frantic wave of magic pulses through me.

My senses reel. My muscles convulse. The mixed scents of our marking and sex sear my primitive brain with pride.

Calli wears my scent now.

"What have you done to me?" I gasp, the world spinning. I struggle to take in enough oxygen so I don't pass out. Ha! That would serve me right. After the fuss I made when Calli blacked out having sex, if I do the same thing it would be a hell of a hit to my man card.

Right. I shut that shit off quick.

Easing out of my new favorite place on the planet, I groan. The loss of connection is horrid. How have the others been able to function? Newfound respect springs to life for Jaxx and Kotah. They've been able to function while not being inside her.

I'm not sure I can.

I help Calli off the little ledge and pull her against my chest. She's spent and clings to me, replete. I hold my hand under the trickling stream of water and cup handfuls of warmth to rinse the milky residue from multiple releases from between her legs.

When we're both clean, she smiles a wry smile. "That was fun. Thank you."

I brush our lips together and chuckle. "You amaze me yet again, Spitfire. Your transition. Your commitment to a world you don't owe a damned thing to. Your dedication to this mating. Your innate fight to survive whatever comes at you. And now this. I didn't think you'd trust me enough to submit."

"This was your turn in charge. I expect to get a turn, too."

I shut off the water completely and help her out into the bathroom and wrap her in a fuzzy towel. When she's dry and looking content, I pull her against my chest and kiss her nose.

"In time. I'll work on letting go, I promise. Be patient with me."

CHAPTER SEVENTEEN

Kotah

*I*t's my deepest pleasure to have Calli all to myself for the day. While Brant, Jaxx, and Hawk work on the investigation of who the Black Knight might be, who the mole in the upper hierarchy of the FCO is, and where our villainous nemesis is housing fourteen gifted young adults, I have the honor of showing Calli my home and introducing her to the members of my pack.

The fact that she's still glowing, literally and figuratively, from her shower session with our avian only adds to her majesty and I'm pleased with the rousing welcome and support she receives from my family.

"Everyone here is so nice," she says as we leave the village proper and head to the clearing to work on her morning training regimen. "It's hard to believe..." She bites her lip and waves the rest of her comment away.

"Hard to believe after meeting my parents? Well... my mother. My father didn't even give us the consideration of meeting with me or my new mate."

She shrugs. "It's his loss. You're amazing and will be an incredibly important member of the fae realm whether you're the next Fae Prime or a Guardian of the Phoenix or just Kotah Northwood a beautiful soul."

I pull her tight to my side and kiss her cheek. With her arm wrapped around my lower back, I could walk these grounds forever and never tire. "I asked Mama to look into any historical reference of the position to see if there's a precedent that could excuse me from serving in my father's stead. Before she retired to raise Jaxx and Laney, she was the head historian of the fae chronicles. Did you know that?"

She shakes her head and smiles up at me.

Midday sun spangles off her long, golden lashes and makes her emerald eyes sparkle like priceless gemstones. "I'm sure between all of us, we'll come up with some way for you to escape life in that palace."

I hope she's right. I draw a heavy breath and release that which—for the moment—cannot be changed. Standing in the center of the clearing, I stop and step behind her. "All right," I whisper into her ear. "Like we practiced. Clear your mind and focus on your phoenix. Greet her. Invite her forward. And then relinquish control to your firebird."

I step back and give her space. "There's nothing to fear. Your animal side is part of you. Allow her the freedom to soar."

Calli shakes her arms out at her sides and goes through her meditation exercises. Deep breaths in, identify her negative triggers. Deep breath out, naming, and expelling them.

She speaks her truths on a whispered breath, and I respect her privacy enough not to listen. When she stills, her feminine frame is noticeably less rigid. She tilts her face up to greet the heat of the noon sun.

The glow of her skin builds. It's as if she's absorbing the fire of the sun and channeling it into her being. Flames burst off her in a whoosh of orange and gold. She stretches her arms out wide and the dancing licks of fire extend off her fingertips.

Movement to my left brings my attention to Keyla and a half-dozen members of our pack who have come out to watch. I raise my fingers to my lips and motion for them to keep their distance. The heat of Calli's flaming female form doesn't burn me like it did before we mated. It's equally as hot, but our bond protects me somehow.

The same won't hold true for them.

Calli's flames grow in length and height, stretching, testing the air until they gather into a rough outline of wings.

That's it, Chigua. You can do this. Believe in yourself.

The flames dance in the air, silhouetting her animal form but not quite taking hold. She tries for a moment longer and then flames out. I pull one of her new fireproof coverup dresses from my backpack and help her shrug it on.

When her head pops through the neck, she looks so defeated it breaks my heart. "No, my love." I pull her to my chest, cup her jaw, and raise her face to kiss me. She tastes of magic and brimstone. "That was great strides closer than ever before. Don't be sad. You're doing amazingly well."

She shakes her head and notices the staring audience. "Oh, gawd. They must be so disappointed. Some phoenix savior I am. I can't even shift."

I wave them closer. They can't get within fifteen feet of us, but by the awe-inspired looks they wear, I know they'll prove my point. "Calli's discouraged because she can't yet shift to her wildling form."

"Oh, m'lady," Tess says, worrying her gnarled and weathered hands. "That was magnificent. A true show of strength and potential."

Logan Silver Fox nods. "Prince Nakotah mentioned that you transitioned from a human life less than two weeks ago. To call your animal forward in that short time is unheard of. It's simply miraculous."

Calli straightens and looks up at me, her eyes sparkling once again. "Really? I thought you were just being nice."

I shake my head. "You are a natural, *Chigua*. If you can do this in two weeks, imagine what you'll do in two more. Believe in your power, my love. And if you can't, we will all be here to believe in it for you.

She looks to my family and their supportive smiles reaffirm my words. Yes. Northwood is exactly where she needs to be. The magic of my home has never let me down—it won't let our phoenix down either.

"Come. There's somewhere I want to take you."

Brant

Working with Hawk and Jaxx is more productive than I expect. By midday, we've uncovered a few thin strands of new evidence leading from the FCO head office to whoever is maneuvering things behind the scenes. All of them are geared to incriminate Hawk, which, I admit he's too smart to leave discoverable if he were the Black Knight.

Jaxx's computer skills are a surprise boon to the team. He doesn't think much of it, but Hawk's impressed and I figure the jaguar must've been a hacker in another life.

Hawk's understanding of company clearance access and the players who could've pulled these strings gets us our pool of suspects. He prints us off everyone's corporate profile and we start taping them up on the wall so we know who the potential players on the board might be.

My contacts and friends among the blue-collar members of the FCO succeed where Hawk's influence ends. Some of the workers feel more comfortable talking to me than to him and there's a lot to learn from watercooler gossip.

By mid-afternoon, we've tugged those loose strands of evidence enough that we're unraveling a tangled web of deceit.

"Have we got a destination for Lukas yet?" Hawk says, muting his call and looking over Jaxx's shoulder. "He's at the Bastion helipad and can move toward a targeted area if we point him in the right direction.

Jaxx leans back from studying the screen of the laptop and makes a face. "West."

Hawk's brow arches. "Seriously? That's what you're giving me? West is rather vague. The fourteen missing kids come from all over the country."

Jaxx nods. "Maybe so, but the companies being contracted for the unexplained construction and renovation equipment are all on the west coast, Olympia, Portland, Seattle. The storage warehouse in your name that you say you never purchased is in Eugene, Oregon. I'm assuming that since Calli's drow biker buddies ran the guns and girls up and down the coast of California, the Black Knight is operating along the Pacific Coast."

My bear lets off a rumble. "That's my home territory."

Hawk puts the phone back to his ear. "We're starting you at a warehouse in Eugene, Oregon. Jaxx will text you the addie. I want a carefully selected covert team on this, Lukas. We're investigating our own people. I don't want this getting back to whoever it is before we catch them in the act."

I signal for Hawk to give me the phone. To my surprise, he doesn't hesitate. "Hey, Lukas, it's Brant. I've got a sleuth-mate with a cattle ranch outside Junction City. It's only fifteen miles from the warehouse in Eugene. You could land without tipping off anyone that you're in the area. Travis and his sons can go into town and rent a couple of trucks and have them waiting for you when you arrive."

Lukas agrees and Hawk gives me the nod to go ahead. I hand

the phone back and pull out my cell. If Darkside assholes think they can fuck around in ursine territory and not face the music, they've got another thing coming. As my Alpha is so fond of saying...

We've got the right to bear arms and the right to arm bears.

Calli

Despite Kotah's pep talk in the clearing, after my washout attempt at shifting, my heart remains weighed down by the failure. Darkside assassins won't pause their plans to give me time to find my inner fire goddess. They'll continue coming at us. Me being the weakest link puts all of them in danger. I don't want them dying to protect me. I want to be strong enough to protect myself and keep them safe too.

My skin remains hot to the touch as I wipe my brow with the back of my wrist. Now that I flamed out and we're hiking through the trails of Kotah's forest, I'm hot and sticky and—I lift my arm and perform a quick sniff test—yep need another shower.

Images of my morning session with Hawk make my girlie parts tingle. He is aggressive and sexy and as much as I enjoyed everything about our time in the shower, I want a chance to explore his body and be tender with him.

He doesn't want tender—I know that.

After what happened with me and my uncle, I didn't want tender either... not until I learned to deal with the abuse. And whether Hawk's abuse was sexual, physical, or mental, somewhere inside him is an angry boy who's so filled with fury he doesn't recognize he deserves to be loved.

"I'm relieved Hawk accepted his place with us."

Kotah's smile is so genuine it fills my heart. "Hawk needs us more than he admits... even to himself. I didn't tell you, but I hugged him yesterday morning before he left for work. He didn't have time to guard his emotions and I sensed the loneliness in his soul."

I squeeze our laced fingers and try to picture Kotah ambushing him with affection. Man, I love my wolf. "You just walked up and showed him some love? How'd he take it?"

Kotah chuckles, looking sheepish. "He stiffened like a plank of hardwood and made a hasty exit. Still, he didn't get angry or tell me not to do it again."

"I wish I'd been there to see it."

Kotah winks and flashes me a playful smile. "Maybe I'll surprise him again when you're there."

"Yes, please do."

We walk in companionable silence taking in the natural wonder of the Northwood canines' home territory. The trees sway overhead spackling us with the dappled light of the mid-afternoon sun. The enterprising rays fight through the canopy of leaves above chasing away the cool shadows of the forest.

As if the universe listened to my earlier wish for a shower, a faint rush of distant water calls. Glancing back toward the village, I wonder how far we've come. Though I'm sure Kotah knows exactly where we are, every tree and every rock look the same to me.

A moment of panic hits and I wonder how we'd defend ourselves if someone attacks. We're alone in the wilds with no backup, no weapons, and no one informed of where we are. We could be ambushed at any moment, and who would know?

I scan the forest and the hair on my arms stands on end.

Paranoid much?

"If someone was perched in these trees watching us," I say, feeling like I'm inviting trouble even saying it aloud, "You and your wolf would know, wouldn't you?

I swallow, listening for anything beyond the birdsongs in the trees and creatures of the hunting and gathering variety.

Kotah turns me in his arms, looking concerned. "I would know, yes. My wolf's senses are heightened beyond those of the others and the animals of the forest recognize me as one of their own. They will warn us if any outsiders trespass."

There isn't an ounce of exaggeration in his tone and my panic subsides. "My very own Dr. Doolittle."

He laughs and starts us walking again. "Hardly. Animals are simply expressive creatures if you take the time to listen to what they have to say. Is it a happy chatter? Are they agitated? Has the world suddenly gone silent and still? If so, why?"

We follow the path for another few hundred yards when the forest transforms and the trees thin. The sound of rushing water grows louder and after a few more minutes spent winding along our forest path, the trees open up.

It isn't a river I heard.

The grotto in front of us is the landing place for the cascading rush of a waterfall. The frothy, white water plummets over a wide crest eighty feet above, hits a platform of large, flat rock sheets, and drains down into an iridescent turquoise pool. From where we stand, opposite the pool, the water sits as still and clear as glass.

Cool mist kisses my face and my skin prickles to life.

Kotah pulls off his shirt, folds it around his glasses, and sets them carefully at the base of the pool. Then, he unlaces the leather ties of his doeskin pants and shucks them down his thighs. I take in the show and then edge toward the water. The outer edge of the pool is bordered by a natural gathering of low rocks. I reach over the rocks and dip my fingers. "It feels like bathwater."

Naked, my wolf steps beside me and pauses with his fingers clutching the hem of my shirt-dress. "It's a limestone pool, rich with fae magic and restorative properties. Join me. I want to show you something."

I chuckle. "When a naked guy says, 'I want to show you something,' it's his cock. It's always his cock."

Kotah laughs, pulls my dress up over my head, and strips me bare. He studies me with the devilish confidence that builds each time we're alone together. He may be a late bloomer, but this guy has endless depths of passion. "I love you, Calli."

I step into his embrace and meet his gaze. When he first said those words a few days ago, it felt too soon to say them back. Sometime in the past week, I've grown to feel at home within his arms. He's my silent support... my number one fan.

How could I not fall for him? "I love you, my sweet wolf."

Our mouths meet in an achingly loving brush of lips and then he steps back and tugs me toward the limestone pool. "And no, it's not my cock. You've already seen that."

CHAPTER EIGHTEEN

Jaxx

*T*he three of us are plowing through a ton of information and making some serious headway when my instincts start firing. Something shifts inside me, my skin feels ultra-sensitive and my blood pulses fast. My cat snarls. Fear. Danger. I pause my fingers on the keyboard and look up to see if the others feel it. Hawk does. He turns his back to the suspect wall and searches the room with a puzzled scowl. Brant seems oblivious.

"You feel it too?" I say to Hawk.

He dips his chin. "Where's it coming from?"

"Where's what coming from," Brant asks.

I save what I'm working on and stand. "You don't feel a distant warning bell going off in the back of your mind? A vibration on the tension of your mating bond?"

Brant shakes his head. "Nope."

Is that because Brant hasn't consummated his bond yet? I'm about to ask when my chest warms, and the mating crystal starts to glow through the fabric of my shirt. I fish out the leather woven chain Kotah wrapped for my crystal shard and hold it up for them to see. "What do you suppose that means?"

Hawk frowns, and swings on his gun holster. "Nothing good. Let's go."

The three of us exit the main house and crest the rise at a jog. It's a strange sensation… an invisible pull to where I need to be. My parents and Laney are chatting with Keyla and Doc outside the two guest cabins where they're all staying.

As we pass, I call out. "Head inside for a bit. Something's happening. Doc, can you—"

"I've got them," Doc says, understanding and rising to full alert. The guy is ex-military and a bear—not that Daddy's a pushover, but I feel better that he's got strength and combat skills on his side.

The three of us continue following the pull and I tuck the crystal back in my shirt to keep it safe. I send up a prayer to the Powers to protect Calli and Kotah until we get to them. My cat is pacing, raging beneath the surface.

Brant's bass rumble provides the soundtrack for our trip.

And Hawk has gone alpha-lethal.

Calli

There's no helping the squeal that slips from my throat as Kotah tugs me into the water. It only feels cold because my skin is molten hot. The underwater inhabitants dart away in streaks of silver, gold, and crimson but are soon hidden below the rising steam that sizzles off the surface. I push forward and follow my wolf deeper into the pool.

Goosebumps tingle up my arms and my nipples tighten into hard peaks. The heated flesh under my breasts feels coldest of all and it takes a few minutes for my body temperature to adjust. Buoyancy takes the weight of my body as I glide toward the center of the pool. It's a peaceful place to swim, and I understand why Kotah wants to share it.

I flip onto my back and flutter my feet until I meet up with Kotah sitting on a rock at the base of the falls. His gaze is locked on my breasts glistening wet in the sunlight and his smile is the most content I've seen him wear yet.

"How do I deserve such a radiant female?" he asks.

I float to where his knees break the surface of the water and right myself to stand between his thighs. He squeezes my ribs with his muscled legs, his flesh sun-warmed and smooth. The silt at the bottom of the pool is silky under my feet and scrunches between my toes as I push up to meet his kiss. "How do I deserve such a loving, passionate soul."

His long, chestnut hair drips cold on my heated skin as we pay homage to our newfound love. His kiss is gentle and content and makes all the craziness and chaos of the past weeks evaporate. "Thank you for loving me, sweet prince."

"The pleasure is mine."

Lost in the solitude of our love-in, I don't pick up on the niggle of a warning when it first pulls for my attention. I don't want anything to interrupt this moment. Life can wait.

Kotah gets to his feet and offers me his hand. He pulls me up onto the rock and together we head toward the falling water of the falls. "Come. What I want you to see is beneath here."

We skirt the heaviest of the falling water and step behind the thundering rush. Kotah helps me navigate the stepping-stone path until we arrive in a rocky cave behind the falls. The stone glitters with iridescence, and while it should be dark back here, it's not. The stone glows bright enough to see perfectly.

I stare at the pink, silver, and green light shimmering along the rockface and my jaw drops. "It's incredible."

Kotah wraps his arms around me from behind and points in front of us. "Look. There you are."

He points at the cave drawings and my mind stumbles on the depictions of a woman transforming into a fiery bird. She's surrounded by her guardians in animal form and fighting a horde of dark figures.

In the next panel, the phoenix hovers in the air in front of a crack in a mountainside. Jagged bolts of lightning shoot off her wings and swirls of magic encircle the opening.

"Wow. Is this what's going to happen?"

Kotah shrugs. "I have no idea. Maybe it's a prediction or maybe it's an artistic interpretation of the legends from centuries ago. I can't say. The thing I do know is that I spent hours upon hours staring at this wall wondering."

I shiver and Kotah's brow draws tight. "Come. You're getting chilled. Let's get you back into the water and the sunlight."

We walk hand in hand out from under the curtain of falling water and back across the rocks. The sun feels amazing on my skin and when we sit to put our legs in the water, I lean back on my palms and soak in the golden rays. "I love it here."

"I'm so glad," Kotah says, his voice deeper than usual.

I open one eye and peek over at him. Naked, with his brown skin shining in the sun and his long hair blowing in the gentle breeze, he's the most beautiful thing I've ever seen.

He draws in a deep breath and smiles, leaning closer. "Do you like what you see, mate? You seem hungry."

With a strength I still don't fully understand, Kotah pulls me from sitting beside him to facing him, straddled over his lap. I chuckle as his erection gets trapped between our bellies. "I'm not the only one who's hungry."

Making out with Kotah sparks all the sweet and sexy in me. Straddling him naked out in the wild brings out more of my wild side. "Isn't this how we started?" I say, clutching his jaw and grinding against him.

"But in Hawk's truck, we got interrupted." Kotah grips my ribs and lifts me enough to position the tip of his cock at my core. As he lowers me, inch by delicious inch, both of us groan. The penetration is exquisite and being exposed with the sun beating down on us makes it all so erotic.

Fully impaled, I draw a deep breath and shudder. Is it fae magic that makes this feel so good? If so, I hope it never ends.

If it's a drug, I'm addicted.

Sharp crumbles of stone under my knees aren't ideal but dismounting until we're somewhere more comfortable isn't an option. Kotah's hands shift from my ribs to cup the weighted mounds of my breasts. Our mouths are locked, my fingers tight in his hair to hold him close.

Our bodies crush together. Even as he penetrates me, I penetrate him. My tongue sweeps his mouth as I ride his cock.

Kotah never seems to feel the need to rush. He savors every sensation, every touch, every pang of pleasure. It's one of the many things that make intimacy with him special.

I pause. The spell is broken as the tingle of some distant warning hits me for the second time. I don't push it away, this time. My phoenix rushes to the fore and I ease back and look around.

"Calli? What is it?"

"I don't know. There's something… I feel it." When my heart searches for what it is, nothing comes to me.

Kotah inhales and lifts me to sit on the stone. Dropping forward, he splashes into the pool and searches the trees beyond. "What sort of *something* do you think it was?"

"I'm not sure." My words haven't completely left my lips when the flickers of light on the surface in front of him shift and swirl as if to dance on top of the water.

My breath catches as the shimmering colors form a circle and advance toward us. Even with the building movement of light, the water remains deadly still. I pull my feet from the water and stand, peering over Kotah's head to the crystal-clear surface beyond. The circle of approaching light seems to frame an object below the water.

"What's that in the water. Kotah, get out of there... I don't like this."

Whatever it is breaks the surface with a small flash and drifts closer. Freaked out, I shuffle back a couple of feet.

So much for being brave.

Kotah doesn't share my scaredy-cat flaw.

The object—floating atop the water surface and moving as if with purpose—gets about a foot from Kotah before I identify what it is.

Okay, wow, so that happened.

CHAPTER NINETEEN

Calli

I twist around, searching for Riley's ghost or a witch or a magic-wielding fae who could've made this happen. No ghost. No witch. Just me and Kotah. The pie-shaped gemstone inches toward him catching the sunlight and casting prisms of color in every direction. Kotah opens the palm of his extended hand.

"Be careful," I say, my pulse racing. "Remember how the first crystal jolted Hawk when it wasn't meant for him?"

"Be at ease, *Chigua*," Kotah says, his voice filled with the unending peace that is my wolf prince. "This one is meant for me. I feel it to the full depth of my soul."

And he must be right because it settles into his hand and his body glows with the same golden aura Jaxx had when he first held his. Golden rays radiate from him like a shockwave of pulsing energy. They hit me first and then shoot across the surface of the pool.

Jaxx, Hawk, and Brant break through the trees and halt to a

slamming stop as the energy pulse hits them and completes the connection.

When Kotah turns to me, he's backlit like an angel of the heavens. When he takes my hand, his bond with the quint locks tighter into place.

"Holy shit," Jaxx says, from across the pool.

"Are you two all right?" Hawk casts a scrutinizing gaze to assess the entire area.

I nod and slip into the water next to Kotah. "We're fine. Kotah found the second crystal."

"Where did it come from?" Brant growls.

I can't take my eyes off Kotah. He was breathtaking before but glowing as he is... I can't even.

I touch the gemstone nestled in his hand. It doesn't have the feel or look of swirling water in it like Jaxx's does. Kotah's is spirit. I don't know how I know it, but I do. It responds to my touch and the power of my phoenix beats strong in my racing pulse. "It came from under the water."

"I saw that, but... how?"

"We don't know," I say, not sure of much in this new world of magic, monsters, and mates. I bite down on my lip. If not for my connection with Kotah and the peaceful ambiance of the falls, I would be completely tripping out.

Hawk

When Kotah and Calli climb over the rock wall of the grotto pool, I take her hand and help her. I'm still a little raw from our shower session this morning and panicking the past ten minutes thinking she was in danger. My visceral need to find her and ensure her safety closes the door to life outside this mating quint. I am fully mated. And as a male of planning and strategic visualization... I hadn't planned on any of this.

My attention snaps back to her when I realize she's staring at me. "Are you all right, Spitfire?" She glances to where I'm still holding her hand and then back. Right. I never released her. The stupid thing is... I don't want to let her go. The concern in her gaze softens and I swear she sees past all my bullshit, right into the dysfunctional heart of me. "Big day, yeah?"

"Yeah."

Still holding my hand, she pulls me to the side and points at her dress. "Can you help me get covered up?"

I don't believe that she wants me to help her pull a tunic dress over her head, but yeah, it gives me a chance to turn my back to the others and focus on her.

It's the weirdest thing... just touching her soothes me.

I gather the hem of the dress and angle the neck hole to help her into it. "You know, I don't think I've ever put clothes on a female before. My expertise is in taking them off." The words are still falling off my tongue when I flinch. "Fuck. Sorry. That was thoughtless."

Calli pulls her hair free from the dress. When she drops her hands, it falls in a golden fan down her back. "I'll take all the firsts I can with you, Barron. It's nice to know there are still a few things I can claim as ours."

It shocks me how stunning she is... no makeup, no airs, no fancy wardrobe. She's nothing like any of the females that came before her. She's sexy, sass, and smartass all rolled up.

I pinch the front of her dress and pull her closer. Leaning forward, I brush my cheek with hers and kiss the shell of her ear. "The most important thing is that you're the first female I ever wanted as my own and the first and last mate I'll ever claim. The rest is a work in progress."

"Good answer," she whispers. "If I didn't know better, I'd even say romantic."

I nip her neck hard enough to make her yelp. "Nice try."

Jaxx

When the five of us return from the waterfall grotto, Laney, Mama, and Keyla rush out with Doc and Daddy to ask about what sent us bolting into the woods. We fill them in on the magical pull on our mating bonds and when Kotah holds up the second mating crystal, Laney's turquoise gaze pops wide.

Blonde and athletic, my older sister fits the mold of our family to perfection. There's no looking at her or me and not realizing we are the sum of our two parents. "And it just rose out of the water and floated over to you?" she asks.

"How did it get there?" Keyla asks.

"Magic, I expect." Kotah holds the crystal between his thumb and forefinger and raises it to catch the light of the sun. "Jaxx's crystal seems to represent water."

"Yours is spirit," Calli says. "I knew it the second I touched it. You are the spirit and the soul of this quint."

"How does a crystal get a power of nature?" Laney asks.

Kotah adjusts his glasses and extends his reach so Mama can get a closer look. "There are three races of pixie that harness the power to enchant crystals with elemental strengths. When I first saw Jaxx's, I thought each crystal chose the guardian with the strongest elemental traits toward its specific characteristic."

"I bet Calli's will be fire," Keyla says.

Kotah chuckles. "That was too easy. But yes, I'm anticipating that Brant will get an earth crystal and Hawk's will represent air. What I'm left wondering, is whether or not the crystals coming to us is the way it's supposed to happen?"

I'm wondering the same thing. "The Fae Council made it sound like we're supposed to venture out on a grand quest to find the scattered pieces of the crystal. If they are enchanted to come to us, that's one less thing to worry about."

Calli laughs. "After the past week of Texas to California to Kansas to North Dakota, it would be nice to let destiny come find us for once."

Brant shakes his head. "Sorry, beautiful. After what we learned this morning, I see a trip to the west coast in the extremely near future. Sadly, our destiny doesn't protect the rest of the world from Darkside agents or the manipulations of the Black Knight."

I cast a glance to Daddy and another wave of guilt hits.

He waves away the concern. "Don't get worked up on my account, son. I know full well that you'd charge into hell with a bucket if you thought it would keep someone you love from burnin'. All's well that ends well."

"Still, now your lives are disrupted and on hold until we get things sorted."

Mama clucks her tongue. "Everythin' happens as it's meant, baby. Until the storm clears, we have the privilege of spendin' time in this paradise with you and your mates. Let us lend a hand here or there if we can."

Laney smiles and moves to take a closer look at my crystal where it hangs against my chest. "All y'all are history in the makin'. If us taking a vacay in an enchanted wilderness helps in the grand scheme, we'll suffer and do our part."

I laugh, pull her close, and muss her hair. "Thank you for your sacrifice, Lane. I love all y'all and am glad you're here."

Kotah

Dinner is a joyous pack affair with a sumptuous pot roast and a celebration that makes me proud. The entire courtyard is lined with torches, lit, and dancing against the night sky, while the village musicians entertain us with a lively playlist that keeps everyone moving to the music and laughing. My favorite part, by far, is that the person leading the charge for the community gathering is my little sister.

"This is the Keyla I love," I say, to Calli and Hawk as we sit on a picnic table and watch the festivities.

Brant and Doc are dancing like fools with anyone who cares to take a spin on the dance floor. Jaxx is dancing with his sister, Laney. And Mama and John are lying all cozy in a blanket atop the rise in front of the guest cabins. They're watching from a distance, understandably shaken from John's abduction.

Calli leans close and bumps my shoulder. "This Keyla is certainly more appealing than the selfish brat you introduced me to at the palace."

"She's got management potential," Hawk says, looking up from the computer he's tapping at. "She organized the pack and had them all smiling as she worked side-by-side to get things accomplished today. She broke down tasks and ran a tight ship. For a girl not yet nineteen, that's impressive."

I nod. "Keyla cares about people. She's much more than the female Mother and the palace make her seem."

The song ends and Jaxx and Brant rush to our table. "Come on, kitten," Jaxx says, taking Calli's hand and tugging her to stand. "Your mates want to see you shake your thang."

Calli giggles all the way to the dance floor.

I catch Hawk watching and decide to continue with my mission to understand him. "May I ask you something?"

The tap-tap-tap beside me stops. "All right."

"When Brant first talked about the five of us mating, you made it clear you wanted nothing to do with mating Brant, Jaxx, and me. Is that still the case or have things changed now that you mated Calli? Would you ever consider mating me?"

He scoffs and shakes his head. "You've never heard of leading with a lob, have you? Straight to hardball."

I shrug. "I wonder how you see this mating playing out. Brant was right when he said there are five of us in this relationship. Even if you stand by your comment to take sex out of the equation, I still want a relationship with you."

Hawk licks his lips as if considering. "I don't know how to answer that, Kotah. I hadn't intended to commit to the quint this morning—" he holds up a finger—"I don't regret it. Don't take that the wrong way. It's just, with Calli, things seem to happen of their own accord. I'll need time to process."

I hop off the picnic table and straddle the seat beside him. His tension rachets but I take no offense. Getting through his emotional barriers will take time and patience. "You're more than the mate of my mate, Hawk. I respect you and what you bring to this relationship. We don't have to be lovers to be true mates, but if you choose to explore that kind of relationship, I will welcome you and look forward to our time together."

Before he answers, I squeeze his arm, send him a rush of loving support, and stand.

He glares. "No more of your seducing touch, kid."

I chuckle and leave to join the others on the dance floor. Avians might be the wildlings known for cunning strategy, but canines are known for stalking and wearing down their prey.

Hawk didn't say no to mating me, so, unless he does, I'm taking that as a yes.

Brant

An hour after Jaxx and I pull Calli onto the dance floor, the music slows, and the celebration starts to dissolve. Kotah's pack knows how to put on a good time and I'm glad his entire life hasn't been the uptight judgment we witnessed at the palace. It'll suck for all of us when he's forced to assume his position as Fae Prime—but it will suck for him most. Sadly, no one has given up, but it looks like that's how things will end.

To give him one night of celebration, we opted not to tell him until tomorrow. There are no loopholes that Hawk or I or Maggie or anyone found to excuse him from serving the remainder of the Northwood term.

"Hey." Calli presses a hand against my cheek and brings my focus back to the two of us swaying under the torchlight. "Why the long face, Bear?"

"Just thinking about Kotah's situation and how ill-suited he is to sustain a life of pomp and politics in that palace."

Calli's smile falls, and she turns in my arms to face Kotah. He's chatting with Logan Silver Fox and Keyla by the dessert table. The three of them are smiling and Kotah is more relaxed than I've ever seen him. "Hey, have you noticed the kid hasn't spouted off a run of regurgitated facts once since we got here?"

Calli nods. "This community and these lands bring out a beautiful side in him. A spark of something special."

"It's a shame we have to watch that spark extinguish."

She blinks up at me and I hate the worry I see brewing in her eyes. "There's still a chance, isn't there? Maggie's looking through historic references for a way to have the guardianship overrule the prime position. And Hawk's got lawyers on it too."

I sigh. "They're in needle in the haystack territory now. I don't think there's much of a chance."

Calli lays her head against my chest. "Maybe his father will hang on and it'll be moot."

I rest my chin on the top of her head and look out on the dwindling crowd. "Twenty-nine years is a long time to hang on. Keyla says the royal physicians give him days, maybe a week. The transfer of power must be done before he dies so the fae realm isn't left without a ruler."

"So, it's happening?"

"Seems so. Silver Fox wants him prepped and ready for tomorrow at sunset."

"It just sucks," she says, dropping her arms from my neck to wrap around me for a hug. "He was happy today at the waterfall... at peace, you know? And then the crystal came to him and it seems like the universe is saying his place as a guardian is his true path."

"I agree, but that doesn't change fae laws. Our system isn't the same as human monarchies. There is no abdication. Like it or not, by this time tomorrow, Kotah will officially be the next Fae Prime."

CHAPTER TWENTY

Calli

*D*espite our best efforts, in the end, there's nothing to be done. Nakotah Northwood, heir to the royal throne of the Fae Prime is out of time and we're out of options. I vote to cut and run. Kotah shakes that off. As much as he doesn't want to rule, he won't entertain any idea that casts a negative light on his pack or the canines as a whole.

I suggest that his mother or his sister become Fae Prime, but that's a no too. He's the male heir and was named at birth as his father's successor. I ask about moving to the next race in line to rule. That's a no too. The elves are next up, and they are in a race civil war over whether the mountain elves or forest elves will rule.

Mama figures that will take a decade or two to settle.

So, it all comes back to Kotah.

Keyla volunteers to help Logan Silver Fox prepare for her brother's transfer of power ceremony and the canines start arriving by the carloads shortly after breakfast. They come to stand witness, saddened by the imminent passing of Kotah's father and politely reserved about Kotah stepping up.

In my mind, they've got it backward.

Kotah is ten times the man his father is. Although, I may be biased because I'm sleeping with one and have never actually met the other.

Regardless, while the others work on an eleventh-hour, last-ditch, Hail Mary, long shot, sliver of a chance possibility to get him out of this, we switch roles and I stay glued to his side as his moral support.

The novelty of me being the phoenix helps to take the spotlight off him. Which isn't much but it's all I've got.

"Has he moved at all?" Laney asks, when Jaxx's family arrives, dressed for the main event.

I look to where my prince sits in an oversized leather club chair staring out at the forest. "Not in the last three hours."

Mama goes over and says something privately to him and kisses his cheek. He nods and stands to hug her.

"Okay, maybe he's coming out of it," I say.

"Well, we'll head over and see y'all in a bit."

The door *snicks* shut after the Stantons depart and Kotah stands before me and gives himself a shake. "The pity-party is officially over. Come. You can help me get dressed."

I take his extended hand and follow. "But first I'll help you get undressed."

That earns me a chuckle. "I'm afraid that must wait. I won't be late. That would give my father a very sharp parting knife to stab me with."

Hawk

I descend the open, wooden staircase into the great room. Brant and Jaxx are dressed and waiting, each of them nursing a drink and standing at the bar. Considering Jaxx has his hand wrapped around the neck of the decanter, I figure we're taking the liquid sedation route. I approve. "Is Calli still in with him?"

Jaxx nods and lifts his tumbler. "Care to join the party?"

"Looking forward to it."

Ice rattles against the cut crystal as splashes of amber push the cubes around in the glass. When he hands it over, I tip it back fast and let the burn take hold while he tops me up.

"It's going to be that kind of night, is it?" Jaxx asks.

"If the clusterfuck fits…"

"It's not right," Brant growls. "It's some kind of antiquated royal slavery. It's fucked up."

I take my time this round and let the body of the Scotch sit on my tongue. "That it does, Bear. That it does."

Kotah

I'm numb for the entire event. As I repeat the words Silver Fox speaks, and hold my palm out to be sliced, and swear my oath on the graves of my ancestors, I think only of the wisdom Mama imparted to me earlier. *In times of doubt, believe in your mates because they believe in you.*

I do. If Calli hadn't resurrected two weeks ago, I would be standing here alone. Instead, standing at my side, I have four strong-willed and passionate mates, my sister, and my new extended family. I'm stronger than my parents think. With my mates beside me, I can do this.

As the ceremony nears its end, the sun sinks behind the pines, symbolically signifying my father's descent from power.

Blossom Silver Fox, Logan's mate, steps before me and I

drop to my knees and tilt my face up to her. "With the strength and wisdom of our people," she says.

The assembly repeats her words.

I swallow and find my voice. "With the honor and fight of a canine."

The assembly repeats my words.

Blossom nods and raises the branding gun to my cheekbone just below my right eye. The mark of the Fae Prime is a Celtic knot and because I'm a canine wildling, and specifically a Northwood, a howling wolf silhouette is added in the center.

My skin burns under the scorching iron but other than the stench of singed flesh, I take no notice. I was prepared to bear the pain in silent strength. No need. Being mated to a phoenix has tempered my body's response to extreme heat.

It works in my favor. I don't feel the pain and the gathered wildlings now think I'm incredibly tough because I don't bat an eye. I'll take the win.

Blossom covers the wound with a healing ointment that will seal the ink, and then she steps back. I rise and stand before her mate. Logan offers me a proud smile and turns to our audience. "May I present to you, His Majesty Nakotah Northwood, Fae Prime in Waiting."

Cue the howls and applause.

"Let the celebrations begin."

~

Calli

"Royalty, bitches!" Kotah empties his tumbler and cants to the side into Brant's broad chest. The bear steadies him and tries to angle him toward the sofa to take a load off, but our wolf is wound tightly and in rare form. He sidesteps the chance to sit and raises his glass in a toast. "Here's to Naquilla, the boy who should've been prime."

He looks at the four of us, frowning when we don't join him. "C'mon, you guys. Toast my brother. I'm sure my parents are toasting him tonight. The son who should've been king."

Hawk curses under his breath. "You had a littermate?"

Nakotah nods, his head bobbing. "Come see."

"Brant, help him," I say, setting my glass down.

"I've got him," Brant says, directing our wolf and keeping him from hurting himself.

He leads us down the hall to a closed-door at the back of the house. When he places his hand on the door, magic snaps in the air and the door unlocks. Kotah fusses with the handle for a bit before Jaxx leans in and opens the way.

From what I can tell from the light seeping in from the hall, the locked room is little bigger than a bathroom and almost as sterile. White marble covers the walls and floors smattered with black plaques with engraved silver plates.

"This is your family mausoleum," Hawk says, approaching the pedestal in the center of the space. Made of black marble it rises from the floor in a smooth cylinder and has a concave bowl at the top with an old-fashioned wick of an oil lamp in the center. Hawk lights the wick and the room glows with the glow of the reflected flame. "Should we be in here?"

Jaxx takes my hand and leans close beside me. "Traditionally, wildlings don't share their dead outside of the family. It is believed that to speak of lost loved ones pulls them from the second phase of their destiny and tethers them between lives. To ensure success in the afterlife, it's best to release them."

"That's sad." Riley is on my mind all the time. Missing her hurts but refusing to think about her or talk about her sounds so much worse.

I release Jaxx's hand and go to Kotah. He's brushing his fingers over a plaque on the far wall and I slide in against his side and read it aloud. "Naquilla Northwood, a male of such worth, the Powers could not wait to claim him for their own."

Hawk squeezes my shoulder and speaks quietly. "That's a common inscription for wildlings who die at birth."

"Except he didn't die," Kotah says, his gaze haunted. "My parents kept him alive in their hearts as the perfect son my whole life." He holds up his glass and chinks it against the plaque. "To you, my brother. The male they believe would've made the perfect Fae Prime."

"Oh, my sweet wolf," I say, stepping in front of him and wrapping my arms around him. "You are not a consolation prize. You're the grand prize."

"Yeah," Brant says, curling around us both. "Fuck 'em if they don't see it, buddy."

Jaxx joins the group hug. "Seriously. Fuck them."

Hawk reaches past my ear toward Kotah's shoulder. "You can't pick the family you're born to—I know that as bitterly as you—but you can pick who becomes your family. Fuck them. You have us now."

As his hand squeezes Kotah's arm, I gasp. A surge of energy lights up my cells and bursts out of me and into them. As our connection strengthens, so too does our power. I'm not sure how I know it but I do. My phoenix lets off a cry of triumph in my head and the growls and purr of my mates tell me they feel it too. It's the first time all five of us have come into contact.

It's the power of our quint aligning.

It's happening.

Hawk

I'm drawn down the stairs in the morning by all the succulent smells of a home-cooked breakfast. Funny. Sleep and I have never been amicable, so I'm accustomed to being the first to rise and shine. I am the proverbial early bird that got all the worms. Not this morning. I find Kotah in the kitchen with Jaxx's mom, the two of them whipping up a lumberjack's feast.

"Morning," I say, sliding onto one of the stools at the breakfast bar.

"Good morning," Maggie says, bright as the rising sun. "What'll you have, dear?"

"Just coffee, thanks. Black."

Maggie—a blonde cyclone of southern strength—gives me a placating gaze and fills a plate. "Nonsense. I won't have my boys heading off to face the world without a full stomach."

It doesn't escape my attention that I have been assimilated as one of her boys. It irked me at the welcome dinner at the Bastion. It bothers me far less now. Reading personalities is my superpower. I know, without trying, resistance is futile.

If I am truly one of her flock, I can at least pride myself in being the black sheep.

Kotah slides a steaming mug of java across the island countertop and brushes my hand when I reach for it. His fingers linger on mine and his soothing touch creeps under my skin.

Today I make a concerted effort not to react and pull away.

As an omega, it's in the very nature of his genetics to need to soothe others. I can't bring myself to deny him that small comfort after yesterday. If caring for us helps him deal with the prime thing, I can bear the momentary contact.

More so, after our magical mate power-up last night in the Northwood mausoleum, it's obvious that connecting with the other mates is essential to us reaching our full potential.

Still, I keep it brief. I break the connection under the guise of needing that first hit of caffeine and offer him a smile. "So, what's your plan from here?"

Kotah nicks a piece of bacon off my plate and leans on the island. "I'm still a guardian, aren't I?"

"As far as I'm concerned, yes."

"Do you consider your duties to Calli and the realm more important than your title and business responsibilities?"

The bottom of the ceramic mug *clinks* against the granite countertop as I swallow. "Not more important but certainly more immediate. I'd like to think I'm learning to juggle both."

Kotah grabs a glass of orange juice and takes a sip. "Then that's what I plan to do too. Lukas shouldn't be out there tracking down our bad guys. The universe entrusted us to handle it. It's time we get back to what's important."

"I doubt it will be that easy."

He rests on his elbows on the counter and leans toward me. "The way I see it, you can help me get up to speed on how to live two lives of responsibility. Keyla can fill me in on what to expect from the palace side of things and you can help me balance it."

Is he serious? "Being the king of the fae realm is a fuck-ton more—"

"Language, dear."

I take in the arched brow of my self-proclaimed Mama-in-law and blink. *Okaaay*, my life has truly flipped on its ass if I have a mother to answer to. I haven't had one since I was five. I rub the tight spot in my chest and bury that down deep.

"My apologies, Maggie," I say, before returning my attention to Kotah. "Being the king of the fae realm is exceedingly more involved than running a corporation."

Kotah shrugs. "But I'm not the fae prime yet and I refuse to give my father one minute more of my freedom than he's already demanded of me. While he lives—I live. My life. My terms. I need you to help me."

I pick up my utensils and start in on my plate. "All right, then I'll clean my plate and then make the arrangements. Have you spoken to your sister about this? If you intend for her to accompany us, she can stay in the background and flag anything you need to know from the palace, but I'll have to hire a couple of security men to—"

"Count me in," Doc says, joining us. "I've got tactical training and can guard the princess."

I catch the possessive flash in the bear's gaze. So, it's like that is it? "All right. I'll assign you as her shadow and give you two men to watch your backs."

Doc nods and steps into the work area of the feast. "Morning, Maggie," he says, kissing her cheek. "Everything smells wonderful. I'm surprised Brant hasn't already…"

"Already what?" Brant says, leading the way as he, Jaxx, and Calli descend the stairs. "Careful what you say, brother. My feelings are tender when my tummy's rumbly."

Jaxx and Calli are both fresh from the shower and share a private smile. Ha. I claimed shower with Calli so thoroughly yesterday I'm sure she thought about me while she was in there with him. Suck it, jaguar.

Calli's gaze meets mine and the heat in those emerald gems triggers my cock to harden on sight.

And so begins another day with my mates.

The plus side… the kid gets all the morning love he needs to shake off last night.

CHAPTER TWENTY-ONE

Kotah

I lean close to the mirror and smile at my reflection. "It's perfect, ladies." Having never worn a concealer foundation before, the fact that Calli and Keyla were able to cover the prime tattoo this effectively boggles my mind.

"I'm amazed it healed and doesn't hurt," Calli says.

"I'm amazed that humans don't use a healing seal," Keyla adds. "They seriously wait days and weeks for their tattoos to scab over? That's barbaric."

Calli laughs. "It's not exactly barbaric. It's annoying and uncomfortable, at most. Humans don't have access to magical balms. They have to tough it out."

I pull back but can't straighten with three of us wedged into the plane's washroom. "Okay, Keyla, out so we can all get out. This room isn't big enough for the three of us and we'll be landing soon."

Keyla exits and Calli and I have enough room to turn and follow. Before we leave the adjoining stateroom, I catch Calli's wrist and pull her back. When Keyla turns, I give my sister a wave and slide the pocket door shut.

Calli arches a brow as I seal us in together. "Something on your mind, wolf?"

I nod and claim her lips. Like always, Calli welcomes my hungers. She meets my kiss, and arches into my touch as I slide my hand under her top and up her ribs. "I wanted to thank you for yesterday. I would've lost my mind if you hadn't kept me sane. I needed you more than I realized, and you were right there with me the whole time. No one has ever been my champion before. You can't know how much that means to me."

With her arms extended over my shoulders, she toys with my braid at the back of my neck. "You're welcome. You deserve a champion. I'm sorry I couldn't do more."

My wolf growls, prowling forward. "There's something more you can do now if you're up for it."

As her attention turns from affection to sex, a ring of flame lights up around the green of her irises. Her phoenix is gaining strength. Soon, she'll be able to set the mythical bird free to soar. "What do you have in mind? Should we pull the couches down into a bed?"

"Sadly, no. I wish this was about us getting naked."

Calli sobers. "Then, what is it about?"

"Brant," I say. Her expression tightens and that's exactly why I feel I must step in. "My love, our bear may seem like an impenetrable tank of a male, but he's hurting. He feels your frustration and disapproval and it cuts him deeply."

She steps back and sits on the sofa. "I *am* disappointed. I won't lie about it. He chose to go after Hawk and undermine the relationship we're building, a relationship I made very clear is a priority to me. I asked you three to drop your animosity toward him and give our broody bird a chance. He lied right to my face and said he would."

I kneel on the ground before her. "I don't think he lied to

you—at least not in his mind. As he followed the evidence of a serious crime, he worried for your safety as well as the success of our mission as guardians. If you believed someone was a danger to me, is there anything you wouldn't do or say to ascertain if that threat was imminent? Would you allow yourself to be talked out of digging further?"

I know I have her on that one because my phoenix mate would never stop if she thought any of us was in danger.

"Just talk to him, *Chigua*. Not about his mistake, but about how despite it, you accept who he is. He's feeling very unsure of himself right now. He's the only one of us not claimed—"

"—That was his choice," she says. "I've invited him to join us a bunch of times."

"I know, but he yearns for a bit of quiet time with you—to be at ease with one another—like our afternoon at the waterfall. Remember how peaceful it was for just the two of us to soak up the sun and be together?"

The warmth of her smile fills my soul. "It will stand out as one of the most magical moments of my life. I look forward to returning and maybe we can finish what we started."

My cock, already hard because of our nearness, pulses behind the fabric of my jeans. "I'll make sure it happens, but this moment is for our bear. Please, take a moment to assure him of his place in your heart. On the outside he's a mountain of a male and indestructible, on the inside, he's a teddy bear."

She nods and squeezes my hand. "Got it."

When I stand before her, she pulls me forward and playfully presses her mouth against the front of my jeans, nipping at the ridge of my cock. "You sure there's nothing I can do for you before we land?"

I laugh. "I love where your mind is and yes, as soon as our day is our own once more, I'll take you up on that offer and return the sexual favor. Right now, Brant's pain is pressing on my heart. Ease him and you ease me as well."

"Okay. Send him back."

I leave Calli, pass Doc and Keyla in the back-lounge, and head straight through to the leather seating area around the small table in the forward cabin. Jaxx, Hawk, and Brant seem to be finished pouring over their maps and plans and are sharing a drink and a bit of quiet conversation.

When I claim the empty seat, the three of them instinctively look back the way I came for our mate. "She's in the aft state-room. Brant, perhaps you could go spend a few minutes with her before we land."

His brow pulls tight. "Am I in trouble?"

"No, but I suggested that you two might benefit from a bit of mate fence-mending."

He rakes his fingers over his skull and through the loose waves of his thick brown hair. "Yeah, I suppose we could." He rises and gently touches the skin on my right cheekbone. "The girls did a good job covering that up, but you know it doesn't matter to us, right? You're just Kotah, our wolf, to us."

My heart stumbles behind my ribs. I press my cheek further into his touch and smile. "And thank the Powers for that. Like I told Hawk earlier. I know who I am and who I want to be. My life. My terms. Thank you for saying it though."

Calli

I sit on the edge of the plush couch and for some stupid reason, I'm nervous. I asked Brant a few days ago if I was screwing things up with him and he assured me I wasn't. I'm not so sure. If Brant's unease is strong enough that Kotah senses it than I should've realized it too and set it right. Maybe I'm not doing as well with this quint mating thing as I thought. It's a lot of balls to keep in the air.

I roll my eyes at myself, considering their balls. I've now seen each of them naked and while Brant and I haven't had the pleasure of anything beyond a few kisses and me tugging on his cock for a brief moment, there's so much more I want to explore with him.

"Knock. Knock." Brant fills the frame of a normal-sized door frame, so the opening in the airplane doesn't begin to fit him. He turns a bit sideways and ducks into the stateroom to join me. "Kotah says I've been called to the principal's office."

I'm about to deny that when he waves away my reaction.

"Nah, I'm kidding. He said that maybe we need a few minutes alone to mend fences."

I shift over on the couch and pat the cushion beside me. When he sits, I climb into his lap and hug him. We sit like that, just holding on, for a long, silent moment. Kotah's right. I feel Brant's tension ease the longer I hold on. I am screwing this up.

"I'm sorry, Bear."

I start to pull back so that I can look at him, but he holds me in place. I'm not a small girl by any stretch of the imagination but tucked under Brant's chin and encircled by the banded muscles of his massive arms, I feel downright petite.

"You have nothing to be sorry for, beautiful."

"No. I do." I kiss the bottom of his jaw and look up at him. I'm accustomed to seeing Hawk's emotions guarded against me, but seeing Brant's defenses up hurts me deeply. Of anyone, he is the most open and easy-going. I thought we'd patched that up after his accident.

"Kotah asked me a few minutes ago, what I would do if I genuinely thought someone, even someone close to me, was plotting to do him and others harm. My answer was simple. There's nothing I wouldn't do or say to find out the truth. And, until I knew the whole truth, I would take every precaution to keep everyone safe. I'm sorry for being angry when that's what you were faced with."

He pulls me close again and holds on. "I'm sorry too. I got caught up in not liking Hawk and when everything pointed to him being a rotten apple, I believed my own worst fears instead of searching for another explanation. The guy can be a real prick, but he's passionate about the fae community thriving."

I squeeze him extra tight and he lets me pull back. Shifting in his lap, I straddle him on the couch and cup his broad jaw in both my hands. "We'll figure out who's manipulating the fae behind the scenes and we'll find those kids. Because of you, we know to look for them. You did good, Bear. You're going to make a wonderful FCO investigator."

I press my lips to his and sigh into the contact. Make love not war is such good advice. It's so much better to be on this side of a disagreement.

"Hey, guys," Hawk says, from the lounge on the other side of the doorway. "We're beginning our descent. Everyone should buckle up."

I give Brant another hug and then pull back. "I guess we should take our seats and join the others, yeah?"

Brant nods. "Yeah."

The two of us take our seats at the front and Kotah takes my hand. He sends a rush of healing energy into our connection and my cells light up. I glance at his piece of the phoenix crystal hanging around his neck and thank the Powers for our wolf. He is our calming essence. He is our foundation. He is our spirit.

"I love you, sweet prince."

No matter what happens in the battles to come or within the quint or with him having to take up the mantel as the Fae Prime. Whatever the magic of the fae universe throws at us, we'll be stronger and ready to face it together because of our beloved omega prince, our wolf, our soul.

~~ THE END ~~

AFTERWORD

Thank you for reading Wolf's Soul. I hope you enjoyed getting to know Calli and her guardians better as they begin to align their quint.
Claim book 3 – Bear's Strength now.

If you are inclined to help a girl out, it would be amazing if you could leave a star rating or review.
If you want more, join my newsletter and be notified when new books launch and for all my news and sales!

ABOUT THE AUTHOR

Author Notes: June 30, 2020

Wolf's Soul marks my thirtieth full-length novel. Yay! Twenty of them are romance fantasy/paranormal and ten are fantasy action/adventure without the sexy times. I love what I do and am so thankful for readers like you who love to spend time with my characters and allow me to do it. It's a win-win.

As I spend time with my Guardians of the Phoenix, I gotta say, I enjoy these four guys: Kotah's soothing sweetness, Jaxx's strong and steady, Brant's smartass banter, and Hawk's broody badassery. I hope these guys give you hours of entertainment and escape.

Find Me

My Direct Sales Site: Shopify
My books
Web page – www.jlmadore.com

Email – jlmadorewrites@gmail.com
Newsletter – JL Series Updates

ALSO BY JL MADORE

JL's Reverse Harem Titles

Guardians of the Fae Realms

Guardians of the Phoenix – Calli's Harem

Book 1 – Rise of the Phoenix

Book 2 – Wolf's Soul

Book 3 – Bear's Strength

Book 4 – Hawk's Heart

Book 5 – Jaguar's Passion

Darkness Calls – Keyla's harem

Book 6 – Dark Curse

Book 7 – Dark Soul

Book 8 – Dark Crown

Guardians of the Crown – Honor's Harem

Book 9 – Honor Restored

Book 10 – Honor Guards

Book 11 Honor Bound

Book 12 – Honor Empowered

Rise of the Amberloq – Lark's Harem

Book 13 – Find the Fallen

Book 14 – Rise from Ruin

Book 15 – Trust and Triumph

Exemplar Hall

Exemplar Hall – Jesse's Harem

Book 1 – Captured by the Magi

Book 2 – Jesse and the Magi Vault

Book 3 – The Makings of a Magi Knight

Book 4 – Clash with the Magi Council

Book 5 – The Unstoppable Storme

Club Sanguine

Book 1 – Moonstone Maelstrom

Book 2 - Sunstone Sacrifice

JL's More Traditional M/F, M/M, or Menage

The Watchers of the Gray Series (Paranormal)

Book 1 – Watcher Untethered – Zander

Book 2 – Watcher Redeemed – Kyrian

Book 3 – Watcher Reborn – Danel

Book 4 – Watcher Divided – Phoenix

Book 5 – Watcher United – Seth

Book 6 – Watcher Compelled – Bo

Book 7 – Watcher Unfeigned – Brennus

Book 8 – Watcher Exposed – Taharqa

The Scourge Survivor Series (Fantasy)

Book 1 – Blaze Ignites

Book 2 – Ursa Unearthed

Book 3 – Torrent of Tears

Book 4 – Blind Spirit

Book 5 – Fate's Journey

Book 6 – Savage Love – epilogue novella

Aliens of Atlantis Series (Sci-Fi)

www.ingramcontent.com/pod-product-compliance
Lightning Source LLC
Chambersburg PA
CBHW020321260626
47156CB00004B/1323